MISADVENTURES

OF A

VALEDICTORIAN

BY
M.F. WILD & MIA MICHELLE

MISADVENTURES

OF A

VALEDICTORIAN

BY
M.F. WILD & MIA MICHELLE

WATERHOUSE PRESS

This one is for Hillary, who beat me out for valedictorian all those years ago. Look at me now!
—M.F.

For the CCHS Senior Class of '95. And to #48 of the South Side Hawks, who not only popped my cherry, but whose sensational tight end still gets me hot and bothered to this day.
—Mia

CHAPTER ONE

C L A R E

My heart pounded so loudly I could hear it. It reverberated through my body, creating an unexpected pulse between my thighs.

We won. *We won!*

I screamed, jumping up and down on the sideline, too overwhelmed with our victory—*Eric's* victory. Eric Hayward was the only player I ever noticed on the football field. Ironically, I don't think he had seen me once in the nearly four years we'd attended high school together. Until his soft brown eyes met mine from across the field. The chaos of the stadium fell to a mere murmur in my mind. Impossibly, my heart raced faster. He shot me a broad, sweet grin that was designed by God to melt teenage girls' panties. My lips parted and curved into a smile.

Then Travis, by far the tallest and best-built player on the field, crashed into Eric with a manly hug. They laughed and hollered with the others, and just that quickly...our connection was broken. A tiny bit of my heart fell, but another part celebrated our brief moment, however fleeting.

I gathered up some of the football equipment from the sideline and carried it into the school. A few minutes later, the team barreled through the doors. I turned, unable to resist the chance to visually appreciate the view of a bunch of hot, sweaty football players.

Eric trailed behind the others. Without his helmet, his sandy brown hair was darkened with sweat and messy from his exertions on the field. Even so, with his flushed cheeks and proud smile, he was irresistible. I couldn't take my eyes off him, and as the rest of the team poured into the locker room, he lingered, until we stood only inches away from each other.

Silence hung in the air between us, but somehow I managed to find my voice. "Congratulations, Eric. You were amazing out there."

Before I knew it, he brought his hand to my face. My heart beat wildly in my chest. First, a look, and now, his touch. Warm and firm. Possessive. Something deep in my core clenched, as I remembered many nights when I would have given anything to have him look at me the way he was looking at me right now.

He bent slightly, and instinctively I reached up toward him, lifting myself on my toes to bring us closer. Presumptuous, maybe, but I wanted that closeness with him, even if he rejected me. But he didn't. Instead, he brought his lips to mine, and his earthy musk filled my lungs. He was tentative only a moment before sliding his palm behind my neck, holding us together. As if I'd had any plans to resist his touch. He probed my mouth with his tongue, and I moaned, because he tasted like lust and confidence...and all the things I imagined someone as untouchable as Eric Hayward would.

I clenched my fists, holding myself back from climbing the beautiful body in front of me. Ten seconds, a minute. I had no idea how long Eric kissed me, but when we parted, I couldn't breathe.

Then I couldn't stop breathing. I might have been hyperventilating, or hallucinating. But damn, I wanted his lips on me again. I wanted his hands. I wanted more of the tease of his tongue on mine and everywhere else. I'd spent so many nights lying in bed, dreaming of the way he'd fuck me—if by some miracle he'd ever notice me in the first place. Heaven help me, I ached for that now more than ever.

His eyes were still bright, energy radiating off him from the win, but his smile had faded. His breath was as ragged as my own. Probably from the adrenaline of winning. It couldn't be from this... from...*me?*

"Damn," he whispered, his gaze trailing over me from head to toe, lighting each part of me on fire. I pressed my hot palms against the cool cinder block wall behind me. Hormones lit up under my skin, causing a fierce ache at the core of me that had never known the touch of a man.

ERIC

My body hurt. The opposing team's linebacker hadn't pulled any punches with that last hit. I drew in a deep breath as the water tumbled over me. I ran my hands over my sore body, the aches a mere whisper of what they'd be tomorrow. Then I soaped up my cock, which was stiffer than I'd ever wanted it to be in a locker room full of guys. But I couldn't get the feel of Clare's lips out of my head. I imagined her lips everywhere and her sweet little tongue sliding up and down my dick.

Clare was a pretty girl but unassuming. I'd hardly noticed her since she'd moved to Ridgeville our freshman year. Her body was always concealed under clothes that were simple and functional—

never stylish or cluttered with brand logos. Now all I could think about was how her faded blue jeans hugged her hips. How her cotton T-shirts molded over her modest but perky tits. Her strawberry-blond hair was a wild tangle of curls, so soft between my fingers when I'd tasted her sweet mouth only moments ago.

I stroked my semi-hard cock, stifling a groan.

Fuck me, that kiss hit me harder than the linebacker had. Where the hell did that come from? And what on earth had possessed me to kiss her in the first place? What was I, a soldier home from war? Pretty much. I'd just thrown the winning touchdown pass in the biggest game of my life. I was eighteen years old and nothing on this earth could have felt better.

I lathered my hair, pulling at the roots to distract me from imagining what might feel better. Like stripping Clare of her frumpy clothes and burying myself deep inside her.

Goddamn. I growled, hastily rinsing off my body. I either needed to get piss drunk tonight or I needed to find Mandy and convince her to give me one for the road. We'd been broken up for a couple weeks. After being accepted to different colleges, we agreed long distance wasn't going to work for us. We had too much temptation as it was. She was sexy and outgoing. And I had a line of pussy out the door at Ridgeville High. I didn't expect college to be much different.

I grabbed a towel, wrapped it around my waist, and went to the girls' locker room, knowing I'd find her there with the other cheerleaders. I had no idea what I'd say, but it'd have to be convincing. She'd already slept with one of my teammates, I figured just to make the point that she was over me. Fuck her. I was over her too. I just needed someone to get Clare out of my head.

And then...there was Clare, carrying an armful of towels across the hallway. She stopped short.

"Hey. Sorry." Her sweet little mouth made the smallest of movements.

I wanted that mouth. Mandy could go to hell, because I was going to have it.

"Coach wants to talk to you," I said quickly.

Her eyes went wide. "He does?"

"Yeah, he said to meet him in his office. Come on."

She hesitated, her soft blue eyes shifting over me, down to where my cock was bulging under my towel, and then back up to my face. Something primal in me was tearing her clothes off in my mind. Goddamn, I just needed to be inside her. Her mouth, her pussy. Something that was Clare.

CLARE

Eric didn't give me much chance to question him. I was utterly confused. A mix of anxiety and desire mingled in the lower part of my belly. Why would Coach want to see me? More importantly, why was Eric, the sexy quarterback who'd just kissed me out of the blue, taking me to him? I didn't care that Eric was leading me by the hand, but I could barely keep up with him as we walked swiftly toward the coach's office. He tugged me into the tiny empty room.

I dropped the towels on the floor by the door and looked around for the coach. "Where—"

"Doesn't matter," Eric rasped. He closed the door and pressed me against it with his hard body. "I fucking need you, Clare. Tell me you want that too."

The breath rushed out of me, and a broken, "Yes," left my lips with it.

He answered with a low growl before he kissed me again. Harder than before. Less cautious and more desperate somehow. I kissed him back, tangling my tongue with his, reveling in his taste. I arched toward him but barely moved because he was pressed against me so hard. And he was so hard.

Oh, God. How was this happening? I couldn't resist any longer. I reached for him, sifting my fingers through his damp hair. He groaned and started pulling at my clothes. I was so wet, aching and pulsing, praying that every touch led to where I hoped it would. With Eric inside me, making me his.

He turned us and pushed me against the coach's desk. My ass rested on the lip of the metal surface while Eric quickly stripped off my shirt and bra. I should have been shy—I always had been. But instead of covering myself, I pushed my chest out, as if to say, *Take what's yours, Eric.*

Heat smoldered in his gaze, and he licked his lips.

"Put your mouth on me," I whispered. All my need and want felt like gravel in my throat. If he sucked my tits I would probably burst into flames, but I didn't care.

Then he did, tugging my hot, sensitive skin into his mouth with fervor. I didn't burst into flames, but a gush of warmth slickened my pussy. I recognized the physical reaction from the fantasies I'd entertained at home in my bedroom, but already I knew I'd never been this wet and wanton before. Fantasy Eric had nothing on real Eric, with his sexy hands and mouth all over me.

I shifted my hips, anxious and antsy for more. He released my nipple with a pop and came back to my lips, kissing me savagely. He slid a hand down the front of my jeans. One slight movement over my clit through my cotton panties had me jolting under his touch.

He paused, pinning me with his stare. "You okay?"

"I want you to fuck me. Eric, I want it to be you. I've never wanted anything this much. Please."

I shouldn't have let on that I was a virgin. I should have just let him take it, but a little part of me needed him to know. My virginity was a gift I could only give once. I'd held onto it for eighteen years, and he was the one I wanted to have it. I didn't know Eric very well, but hopefully he deserved it and would make it good for me. How could someone as hot as Eric Hayward be anything but a dream in bed?

We weren't in bed, but I wasn't about to be picky. Never acknowledging my invitation with words, he worked my jeans off my hips and kissed down my thighs. Then the door swung open.

I sucked in a panicked breath. Eric and I were up to no good, and by the shocked look on Coach's face, he seemed to recognize that instantly.

I considered covering myself, but instead I stood proud. I'd ranked at the top of my class all four years at Ridgeville, but somehow Eric Hayward on his knees ready to fuck me silly felt like my crowning achievement.

Instead of yelling and telling us to get dressed, Coach walked in slowly. Only when he stepped to the side did I realize he wasn't alone. Travis's large frame appeared behind him. His jaw fell and his lascivious gaze seemed to zero right on the wet panties that were the only scrap of clothing covering me. The door slammed shut and

Travis shot a nervous glance at Coach, who showed no emotion or inclination as to what he would do next.

Eric stood, his substantial erection tenting the terry cloth of his towel. Oh, how I wanted to rip that towel off. Fantasy Eric was well-endowed, and I just knew the flesh and blood version of Eric would be too.

"Don't stop on my account," Coach said sharply.

"Sorry, Coach. We got a little carried away after the win." Eric didn't look as regretful as his words let on. Maybe he was expecting Coach to let us off the hook. Eric was the star of the team, after all.

Coach crossed his arms and leaned against the wall. "Travis was the one who scored tonight. If he hadn't caught your pass, you wouldn't be celebrating right now."

Travis and Eric shared a look, but I didn't know what was passing between them. All I knew was that I was horny as hell, and I needed Eric's cock like I needed my high school diploma.

Eric finally spoke. "What are you saying, Coach?"

"Not very sportsmanlike not to share, Hayward. You boys played hard out there."

The boys said nothing, and Coach glanced in my direction.

Energy—fear and anticipation and a breath I was holding too long—lodged in my chest. Was he serious? Travis's stance was wide, his gaze shameless. He adjusted the hard bulge in his jeans and ran his other hand through his damp blond hair. He must have just showered too.

Two smoking hot football players? A moment ago I only had to worry about being good enough for Eric. I wasn't sure how I'd satisfy them both, being so inexperienced myself. Eric must have read the hesitation in my expression because he squared his body with mine and teased his thumb up the seam of my pussy, flicking harder over my clit through the cotton. He leaned down, his breath warm against my ear.

"We'll make it good for you. I promise, Clare. I want to see you come so fucking bad."

I exhaled and struggled to fill my lungs again. I nodded, licking my lips nervously. The warm brown of Eric's eyes soothed me, and I imagined that I saw affection in those beautiful depths. I believed in that moment I could trust Eric to take care of me.

"Okay." The word left me shakily, but I had a feeling I'd be too busy getting fucked six ways from Sunday to say much more tonight.

Coach cleared his throat, a sudden sound that seemed to snap the rest of us from our lusting and longing. I shifted my gaze from Eric's and met Coach's eyes, which were unreadable.

"I'll leave you to it then," he said, before turning to leave.

The door slammed shut behind him, leaving a thick silence between the rest of us. Then Travis went to work unfastening his pants, and my heart jumped into a rapid beat. Eric laid me down lengthwise on the desk and took my panties off. "Her pussy is mine," he muttered roughly.

Travis smiled in acknowledgement, and a wonderful feeling of surrender softened every muscle in my body.

Eric finally rid himself of the towel, revealing the embodiment of every fantasy I'd ever had. His erection was long and gloriously thick. I was terrified and thrilled all at once. He lifted his chin toward Travis. "Condom?"

Travis smirked and pulled his wallet out, withdrawing two

condoms and handing one to Eric. "Good thing I always carry plenty."

Eric sheathed his gorgeous length and began fingering my pussy, slipping into my wetness as if he was testing me. Travis stroked the outline of his cock through his boxers with one hand and brushed his thumb over my lips with the other. "Wow, you're really beautiful, Clare. How did it take me this long to notice?"

He surprised me by lowering down and kissing me gently. He smelled different than Eric. Spicier, with a hint of cologne.

Then I felt Eric's cock nudging against my entrance. I sucked in a breath, fear suddenly overriding my desire. I curled my hands over the edge of the desk, holding on, not knowing exactly what to expect.

ERIC

My body raged with lust, but more than anything, I wanted to make this good for Clare. I pushed a little farther into her wet heat, feeling the resistance of her virginity against the head of my cock.

She was tight, but I wasn't sure if that was desire or fear making her clutch at the tip of my aching dick. Her fingers were curled around the edge of the desk while Travis kissed her. I released her tense fingers and took her hand in mine. I wanted her to hang onto me, not a piece of metal, as I was obliterating her innocence.

I gave her shallow strokes until she relaxed. Travis was at her neck, sucking at her skin. I envied him, getting to taste her and breathe her in. Finally she sighed, her muscles going lax again. Now. I needed to take her now.

I pushed through that invisible barrier, and my eyes rolled back. I should have stopped and given her time to acclimate to me, but she felt too good, too fucking perfect. I thrust again, going as deep as her body would let me this time. Her grip on my hand was firm, but Travis was at her tits now, sucking and massaging each one until she moaned.

I squeezed her hand, silently asking her to tell me if it was too much. She threaded her fingers through mine and whimpered with pleasure. That was enough to spur me on.

I fucked her in steady strokes. Each one tested my resolve to hold out and make this good for her. I'd promised her I would. I couldn't fail her, especially since she'd been a virgin until a moment ago. But for the first time I was grateful that Travis was here as backup if I lost control. She'd get hers, one way or the other.

Travis was stroking his dick now, and I was wondering where he planned to put it. I recognized the lust in his gaze when he lifted his head.

"Turn her around, Hayward. Let me have some of that ass."

I cursed silently. I didn't want to fucking share her, but I knew I probably had to. I pulled Clare up into my arms. She melded against my chest, her eyes soft and hazy.

I kissed her softly. "You okay?"

I couldn't hide the concern in my tone. Travis would have to go home unsatisfied if that was what she wanted. But where I expected fear in her eyes, I only saw soft resignation.

She sighed against my lips. "I'm good, I promise."

"Thank fuck," Travis breathed, stroking his cock a little faster and stepping back.

Carefully I turned us so I was lying on the desk and she was straddling me. I shoved my cock deep into her tissues again, and she sighed like I belonged there.

Then Travis was behind her, lubing her with his spit and lining himself up to her ass. I held her tight, bracing her for what was about to be another intense invasion.

I flashed him a warning look, silently demanding he be gentle with her. He nodded, and then he slowly claimed her. I held her tight and kissed her fiercely. She tensed, and her high-pitched moan was muffled between our mouths. Then she relaxed a little and shifted her hips like she was experimenting with this new situation.

The pressure was intense. I wasn't thrilled that Travis's dick was in my girl, but it did take the pleasure off the charts. We took turns, thrusting, whispering praises to her. Because she was incredible, taking both of us like a champ.

"Yes, oh God, yes." Her voice was shaky and desperate. She was so close. Fuck, so was I.

Then we were merciless, going at her with all we had. She screamed, shaking from head to toe, and Travis stilled his motions with a strangled sound and one last punch of his hips.

I still hadn't come, but the orgasm was crawling up my spine.

Travis slipped out of her, and stumbled back. "Damn, Clare..."

I took that opportunity to drive into Clare harder and faster until she clenched around me. Nothing had ever felt this good. "Fuck, yeah. Come for me. One more time. Squeeze my dick the way you do, Clare."

A broken cry left her lips, and a second later, I came hard, pushing up into her as far as I could go. She collapsed in a weak pile against my chest.

Travis trashed the condom and zipped his pants up. "Clare, it's a goddamn shame we didn't find you earlier. We were ten and O. We could have celebrated this way every time. Your ass...fuck."

I let out a tired exhale. "Enough, Travis. I'll catch you later."

"Sure thing. I'll see you later, Clare," he said with a wink before leaving us alone.

No, he goddamn wouldn't. I stayed nestled inside her, my arms holding her against me.

"What are you thinking about?" she whispered, feathering her fingertips down my cheek, her light blue eyes wide and still so innocent.

"I don't want to let you go yet," I admitted, too blitzed from coming so hard to think twice about what I was saying.

But what did it matter? Mandy was in the past, and before long we'd graduate and be off to college, on to a completely different life than the one we'd known here. Maybe for the first time in my life I could say what I was really thinking and own it.

"Feels good to hear you say that," she murmured, like she wanted to say more or hear more.

"Not as good as this felt." I thrust up inside her gently. Bliss. Her pussy was pure fucking bliss.

As she bit her lip, her cunt rippled down my length. "That felt good too."

I fought the urge to drive into her again, to keep her riding me until I was fully hard again. Keeping my grip firm on her hips, I stilled and breathed deeply through my nose.

"Were you okay with...Travis? I didn't plan for things to play out that way when I brought you here."

She shrugged. "It was fun. I mean, it was really intense. The sensations. And even though we weren't alone, somehow I felt like it was just us."

"I couldn't take my eyes off you. I've never enjoyed watching someone come as much as I did tonight with you. You're incredible."

Silence fell as I realized how that must have sounded to her. I'd fucked plenty of girls, but I was the only man, other than Travis, she'd been with in any way. I didn't know how else to tell her how special she was in the current context, though. I cursed inwardly and then decided not to worry about it. We'd had fun. She'd come. More importantly, somehow through all of this we'd found each other... discovered what sex could be like between us. Two strangers who wouldn't have given each other a second glance before.

I finally lifted her enough to pull out. I'd grown softer, but not completely. I could have fucked her for hours...all night long if we had a more private place. But I had to get back to the guys to finish celebrating with them. And she'd be sore if I took her as long and hard as I wanted to. I could hardly believe this had been her first time, but I was glad that if anyone had shared the experience with me, it was Travis. He loved women as much, if not more, than I did.

I was already replaying the night in my mind, tucking a dozen intoxicating moments into my memory for later. As I finished dressing, I felt her gaze hot on me.

"What are you thinking about?" she asked.

"Nothing, babe." I forced the goofy grin off my face. I went to her and kissed her one last time. One last memory... "I'll see you around, okay?"

Warmth glittered in her pretty blue eyes. "See you around."

CLARE

After Eric left, I dressed quickly. Oddly, I didn't feel quite as dirty as I should have. I liked the idea of Eric's sweat against my skin. Even Travis's. He smelled different than Eric, felt different. And his mouth... I flushed at the thought.

Then I started to wonder what Eric's mouth would feel like on my pussy. Would he plunge his tongue and fingers inside me if given another chance? My belly clenched low, and I almost regretted my reaction to the vision. I'd be craving those sensations until...until we found a chance to meet again. If he truly wanted to, maybe that would be soon. Maybe before the school year was over. I wouldn't feel this way again until I found someone else to ease that ache.

Already, I knew Eric was the only one I wanted inside me again. Unless he happened to have Travis with him. Then I'd probably have to consider them both.

I stepped out into the hallway, and closed Coach's door behind me with a click. Outside of the office, the brief haven where I'd lost my virginity and shared a few precious moments with the unofficial love of my life, everything felt different. The fluorescent ceiling lights illuminating the hallway seemed to highlight what I'd done the way a black light revealed the secrets of a crime scene. My wilted, slightly damp clothes. My unruly hair. The sheen of dried perspiration against my skin. Would someone be able to see it on me, what I'd done?

I'd risked everything. My school record. Maybe college. My reputation, though it was socially unremarkable, would have become remarkable in all the wrong ways. But I'd gone into this willingly. More than willingly. All the years of secretly loving Eric had culminated with this night where my fantasies could play out. And so many of them had.

A door opened down the hall, and a rush of female voices and bodies started toward me—the cheerleading squad, dressed in their stylish clothes. Their hair was done up in tight buns and ponytails, their faces vibrantly made up. Mandy Keller was at the forefront, leading the rest down the hallway toward me. I leaned against the office door, forcing my body flat against it, wishing I could disappear inside that small haven again until they passed.

Mandy and the girls passed me one by one. A few of them gave me bored sidelong glances. Mandy didn't. I didn't exist to her, and for good reason. She was beautiful and popular. At the top of the desirable female food chain at Ridgeville High. That's why she'd been with Eric. Yes, Eric had had her. I couldn't deny that was true.

He'd fucked her too.

He'd seen her come.

The door at the other end of the hall closed behind them, leaving silence. All I could do was smile.

CHAPTER TWO

CLARE

Six months later...

"Pomp and Circumstance" blared through the speakers in the auditorium as I led the senior class down the long center aisle. Once we reached the end, the line parted and my classmates took their seats among the rows of metal folding chairs. Leaving them, I headed up a small set of stairs, taking my appointed place on stage. While everyone settled into their chairs, I braved a nervous glance at my classmates, my focus settling on the only face I'd thought about in months.

Eric's.

Sometimes I wondered if it had all been a dream. It had been six long months since we parted ways in the coach's office, but I could still remember how incredible his thick cock felt thrusting inside me, fucking me into a blissful oblivion. I had given him my innocence, and in exchange, he and his best friend had introduced me to a world of pleasure unlike anything I could have ever imagined.

I couldn't fathom how anything could ever top that. The delicious memory of the way he and Travis had filled me up was enough to make my pussy constantly ache for another round. But we were graduating now. I wasn't sure what the summer would hold before we all left for college.

While Principal Morris addressed our senior class, I gave one last look at the note cards in my hand. I didn't want to take any chances. This speech was simply too important for me to mess up.

Suddenly, all the hairs on my arm stood on end as a rush of energy hit me. Holding my breath, I slowly lifted my head and glanced out across the crowd.

One look.

That's all it took for Eric Hayward's potent stare to pin me to my chair.

"It gives me great pleasure to introduce this year's valedictorian, Miss Clare Winston." The principal announcing my name severed our powerful connection.

Rattled with nervous energy, I stood and smoothed down my gown. As I crossed the stage to stand behind the podium, I could feel Eric's dark gaze follow, stripping me naked with his eyes. Shuffling my note cards in front of me, I forced a smile, took a deep breath, and addressed the full auditorium. Through each word I spoke, I silently coached myself not to look at him. But the longer I stood, the harder it became. Turning my head, I gave in to the overwhelming temptation.

Once my eyes locked to his, the large audience of parents and students seemed to fade away. A knowing look passed over his features, making every inch of my skin prickle with desire. When he slowly licked his lips, my clit throbbed, aching for his mouth.

A heated blush spread across my body. Gripping the sides of

the podium, I braced myself, feeling my knees weaken. I took a deep breath and continued on with my speech. As I delivered the last line, I looked directly at Eric.

"And so I leave you tonight with this challenge, as you set out into the world. Never stop chasing your dreams. One day, they may come true."

I realized now the whole thing could have referenced Eric and my feelings for him. He was my dream, but he was also an impossible future.

The sudden applause in the room broke our hypnotic spell, robbing me of our special connection. Keeping my head down, I took my seat beside the other speakers and focused on the scratched wooden floor in front of me.

Had he known I was talking about him? Could we ever be together again the way we had been?

The rest of the ceremony passed in a blur. I barely remembered lining up to receive my diploma. When we were done, loud cheers erupted and my classmates celebrated by throwing their caps high into the air. I didn't bother joining in. Their gleeful celebration was just another painful reminder of how I never quite fit in at this school.

The once-calm scene suddenly became chaotic as families made their way from their seats to find the graduates. I scanned the large auditorium and spotted Eric just as a bright flash illuminated his handsome face. His family beamed with pride as they posed for pictures and captured the moment. More pain radiated through my chest.

No one had come to congratulate me. My father's date with a bottle of Tito's trumped watching his only daughter graduate at the top of her class. My mother's sudden death in a car accident three years ago had shattered him. In a way, I lost both of them that night. For a long time, I'd held out hope he would heal enough to be a parent to me, but that never happened. Even though I'd learned to accept being disappointed, the pain of his absence tonight was almost unbearable. Unforgivable.

"Clare!" Megan, one of my best friends, ran toward me and threw her arms around my neck. When she pulled away, she was still bouncing with excitement.

"We did it! We're done with this miserable school forever."

I couldn't help but laugh at her little dance. She grabbed my hands and squeezed, squealing with delight.

"Just think, four weeks from now, you and I will be lying on the beach. No parents. No rules. Aren't you excited?"

Excited wasn't the word. I'd been counting down the days until our summer getaway for months. Booking the trip had taken a huge cut out of my savings account. I didn't care, though. I would just have to work extra hard this summer at my waitressing job. Hopefully, if the country club clients tipped the way I expected, I'd have my balance built back up in no time at all.

Just as I was about to speak, Megan's mother shouted her name and waved her over.

"Shit, I've got to go back to my family. You're going to Travis's graduation party later, right?" She raised her eyebrow at me.

I hesitated with my answer, chewing on my bottom lip as I thought about what to say. The entire school had been buzzing about Travis's party all week. But after what had happened between us, I didn't know how to act around him. How would I start a conversation after what we'd done?

Megan would kill me if I said no. I wanted to tell her everything that had happened, but this wasn't the time or place for those kinds of confessions.

"Uh...yeah, I'll probably stop by for a little while," I lied. I had absolutely no intention of going to that party.

"Yay! I'll see you there." She gave me another hug before running back to her waiting parents.

When I scanned the room once more, I caught Eric staring at me. His smoldering gaze sent another wave of desire rushing through my body. Excitement filled my chest when I realized he was heading toward me. But before he could cross the aisle, a pair of arms flew around his neck. Mandy was suddenly between us, pulling his face to hers, tugging at his sandy brown hair as she kissed him full on the lips. Stunned, I blinked hard, as if the image before me would somehow disappear like a mirage. But it didn't. My chest tightened and I looked away, not expecting their kiss to hurt me so much.

It wasn't like I didn't know their history. They had broken up earlier in the year, not long before our little rendezvous. They weren't officially an item, but seeing them touch like that made me think she still meant something to him. I'd hoped for another chance to be with him, but now I realized how foolish I had been to believe I'd ever get that chance. Some part of me always knew he'd never settle for someone like me when he could have a bombshell like her. God, I'd been such an idiot to think I ever stood a chance.

Dropping my head in defeat, I hurried in the opposite direction and shoved open the exit door. I wiggled between people gathered there and turned down the adjacent hallway, grateful to find it vacant. Now that I was alone, I could finally let out the tears I'd been holding back. I was so upset, I didn't even pay attention to where I was going. I just kept walking deeper into the school. As I rounded the next corner, my body collided with a solid wall of muscle.

"Clare?"

Through my tears, I looked up into Travis's handsome face. His spicy smell invaded my nose, settling me instantly. I hadn't forgotten his scent.

His brows furrowed. "Are you okay?"

His question hit me hard. I wasn't remotely okay. I was alone on the most important day of my life. I wanted to forget everything. There was only one way I could do that. I eyed him hard, allowing the idea to swirl in my head.

Fuck Eric Hayward.

Without hesitation, I grabbed hold of Travis's graduation gown and pulled him toward me, crashing my lips to his just as Mandy had to Eric. At first, he didn't return my kiss, and I worried that my forcefulness had caught him off guard. But as quickly as the doubt entered my mind, his erection was pressing against me, confirming that he was definitely on board with my plan.

I dropped my hand and cupped his hardness to show him how greedy I was to have it. Travis groaned into my mouth, shoving me back against the wall as he deepened our kiss. I wanted more. I wanted him to make me forget the person I really ached for. Eric. I was playing a sick and twisted game I knew I would probably regret, but right now I needed to come more than I needed to breathe.

Before I could blink, Travis had pulled me inside a nearby storage closet, slamming the door shut behind him. Through the darkness we fumbled, stripping off each other's gowns and the clothes underneath. The only bit of light was what seeped in beneath the door, revealing my ripped panties beside my feet. Honestly, I was relieved that I couldn't see Travis's face. It made it easier to pretend he was Eric. I knew that would be the only way I could get through this.

I jerked the leather belt free from his waist and worked frantically to unfasten his pants. Using both hands, I forced them down with a wildness that surprised even me. Desire fueled my actions. I dropped to my knees, feeling blindly for his cock. He jerked in my grasp as I worked my hand up and down his shaft. The sounds of his appreciative moans only made the experience in the dark room more erotic. My strokes grew stronger as I grabbed the base of his long cock and squeezed his delicious girth with my fist. No wonder he'd made me come so hard.

"Clare." He panted, pulling away from me. "Are you sure about this?"

By way of an answer, I took his thick length into my mouth, sucking with all my might. As if caught off guard, he stumbled back a step.

"Goddamn, baby," he muttered. Then he came close again and placed his hand on the back of my head, urging me to take more of him.

I eagerly complied, feeling his length hit the back of my throat. The hint of his salty essence on my tongue made me moan in delight.

He gasped and pushed my shoulders back. When he pulled me up, my mouth made a loud popping noise as the sealed suction was broken.

Travis fumbled at his pants on the floor and then seconds later I heard the crinkling sounds of a condom wrapper. Thank God he was using his head. I certainly wasn't.

He firmly gripped my waist, turning me around as he yanked my ass back toward him. I slapped the wall in front of me, barely managing to catch myself before my head hit. Travis slid his hand around to my front, gliding across my mound, inching toward my pussy.

"Mmm. You're fucking dripping for me, aren't you?"

Without waiting for an answer, he sank his long fingers inside me, stealing my breath as he fucked me with them. Just as I was about to come, he removed his hand. A small whimper left my lips at the empty feeling.

Then, I felt the heat of his breath at my ear. "Don't worry. I'm gonna get you there, baby."

He slapped his cock against my ass twice before lining himself up with my soaked opening. I ached to have him inside me...for him to relieve the throbbing that had been building for months.

"Please hurry," I begged, my desperation growing by the second.

My lower lip trembled as I felt each delicious inch of him stretch me, filling me so deeply I thought I would cry from sheer pleasure.

"Jesus Christ," he gasped, sinking in deeper. "No wonder Eric kept your pussy all to himself."

I winced, because I didn't want to think about Eric. Instead I focused on Travis, on the pleasure he was giving me as we fell into a perfect, hard rhythm. The erotic sounds of our bodies slapping against one another drove me closer to the edge. Travis's forceful thrusts grew more feral, each push taking me closer and closer to the blissful edge of orgasm. Desperate to ride it out, I pushed my ass back into him. When I felt the tip of his cock hit my cervix, I rolled my eyes into the back of my head. Dear God, I could practically see stars.

"So. Fucking. Tight."

His loud growl as he came only intensified my own climax. I couldn't stop shaking as he collapsed against my back. Together, we sank to the concrete floor.

Several moments passed in silence, our bodies warm against each other, only our ragged breathing filling the tiny room. The heavy smell of sex permeated the air, clinging to my skin with the memory of Travis's hands on me.

Part of me regretted what had just happened, but a deeper part of me fucking loved it. Travis had just proven to me that my options were limitless.

ERIC

When I came to my senses, I pushed Mandy away from me, instantly breaking our kiss. Using the back of my hand, I wiped my mouth, disgusted by the thoughts that rushed through me. There was a time when all I did was dream about kissing those cherry-red lips. But that was before they'd been wrapped around the cocks of half the fucking football team. The bitch had just been with Travis last week, for fuck's sake. I didn't want my best friend's dick on my mouth.

I narrowed my eyes. "What the hell was that all about?"

"Oh, come on, Eric. Don't be like that. Let's go somewhere we can celebrate for real." She slid her hand over my chest, inching downward. I grabbed her by the wrist and pushed her hand away.

"Not interested." I glanced around the auditorium full of people, searching for Clare, but she was gone. Damn it. I knew she'd seen Mandy kiss me. I could only imagine what she was thinking.

Using my arm, I pushed Mandy to the side and ran toward the nearest exit. I had to find Clare. Suddenly I was furious with myself for having waited so long to get to her again. But, just as before that one incredible night, our lives so rarely intersected. She was in all the honors classes, constantly busy with her work. She never frequented the parties that I went to, and she lived on the other side of town. We lived completely different lives, in and outside of school. But none of that mattered now. School was over, and I was done waiting. I needed to taste her, to feel her come apart in my arms again.

I used my height to my advantage, looking over the crowd for her. When my gaze landed on Clare's best friend, I maneuvered through the sea of people until I reached her.

I tugged at her elbow to get her attention. "Hey."

Megan's eyes widened. Her expression conveyed complete shock that I was talking to her. I studied her reaction, wondering if she knew what happened between Clare and me.

"Oh, hi, Eric," she stuttered, flushing as she tucked her red hair behind her ear.

"Have you seen Clare?"

"Yeah, I thought I saw her go that direction." She pointed toward the long hallway that led back into the school. It didn't make any sense to me why she'd go that way, but this was the only lead I had on her.

"Okay, thanks."

I left Megan and headed back. As I turned down the quiet

hallway, I realized this was probably the last time I'd be in this school. When I passed the large trophy case, I paused and stared through the glass at the tall championship trophy our team had won last fall. I could still remember how incredible it felt to have thrown the winning touchdown of the game. The cheers would echo in my ears for the rest of my life. It didn't seem possible that all that was all over now.

I'd almost given up my search for Clare when I heard a door close nearby. Hope once again filled my chest. Picking up my pace, I turned the corner. Then I stopped dead in my tracks. Travis was fumbling to fasten his pants. Even from this distance, I couldn't help but notice the huge satisfied expression plastered across his face.

I remembered countless times I'd seen my best friend doing the same thing after a hookup. Travis Whyte was the epitome of a manwhore. He craved pussy like it was fine cuisine. I shouldn't have been surprised he'd score some at his own graduation. But something about his expression gave me pause.

Taking a step forward, I was just about to call his name when the door opened behind him. I bit my lip, waiting to see his latest conquest. As if in slow motion, the girl's face lifted, revealing information I wished I could forget. But I couldn't unsee it. My heart plummeted as our eyes met. Her name fell from my lips in a painful whisper.

"Clare."

CHAPTER THREE

CLARE

The air went from stifling to frigid as I passed from the country club's shaded balcony into the air-conditioned dining room. While Ridgeville's youngest club members spent their time at the golf course throwing back cocktails in the summer heat, the wealthier and more refined patrons lunched at white-linen-covered tables overlooking the expansive greens. As a server working both areas, I had the benefit of both views, which I may have enjoyed more if I hadn't been working nonstop for the past few weeks since graduation. I was determined to earn back the money I'd spent on my upcoming trip with Megan. Plus, I had to save plenty for my first year at college. As a result, I'd been taking every shift I could get.

"Get the lead out of your ass, Clare," my boss barked.

Late thirties, prematurely balding, and shockingly single, Greg had suggested last week that I wear lower-cut tops to help with tips. He was a sexist jerk, but he'd been right. I traded in the standard white cotton logo T-shirts for a scoop-neck version. With that adjustment and the right bra, my tips had nearly doubled that week.

I ignored his berating and hustled to the bar to fulfill another drink order. I caught my breath while the bartender worked on my list of elaborate cocktails. I swept my hair off my neck, enjoying the brief reprieve from the heat. I'd been wearing my hair down, since the big tippers seemed to like that too. Never mind that my curly hair was an epic frizz. They were probably too busy looking at my tits to care.

I'd never paid much attention to my looks, but in the months since I'd lost my virginity to Eric and his best friend, Travis, my awareness of my body had completely transformed. I was no longer the same quiet and introverted Clare Winston whose only claim to fame was beating out the GPAs of my fellow classmates at Ridgeville High. Now, I was Clare Winston, the girl who'd had the two hottest guys on the football team—at once.

My heart melted every time I thought about Eric Hayward, but the butterflies quickly dissipated when I remembered Mandy's lips on him and the way I'd thrown myself on his best friend to ease the pain afterward.

I hadn't decided yet if I regretted hooking up with Travis. The whole graduation day had been rotten, disappointing from start to finish, with the exception of the incredible orgasm Travis had given me in the storage closet. But the look on Eric's face when he caught me afterward was tattooed on my memory, unwilling to fade. I couldn't believe that he might care about my little infidelity. It wasn't like we were dating. I was shocked he even knew my name before we'd hooked up.

I closed my eyes, reliving a sliver of our time together. Eric's tenderness. The fire in his touch. The way he looked at me made me feel like what we'd shared could have been special despite my inexperience and his popularity. I shook my head and tried to focus on the task at hand. I had a few tables that still needed orders taken. I couldn't let my thoughts keep wandering to an impossible dream, a fantasy with no future.

As I forced that thought from my mind, I heard a familiar voice. "Clare. Is that you?"

I spun, and my heart nearly exploded. Was it possible that Eric Hayward had grown even more attractive over the past three weeks? He pushed back the sandy brown hair that feathered down onto his forehead and worked his gaze over me. As much as I relished the hunger in his eyes, I hated the hard look that came next. Disappointment, and maybe a shred of anger. He tensed his jaw as he approached. His presence felt imposing, from his broad shoulders all the way down to his toned legs. The muscles under his polo shirt twitched as he shoved his hands into the pockets of his shorts.

My mouth fell agape as I searched for words. "Eric...I wasn't expecting to see you here."

"My parents have been members here since before I was born." His tone was hard, cutting through me.

I stared down at my canvas shoes. The formerly white fabric was stained now from weeks of hustling drinks and food to my wealthy clientele. Never mind not being in Eric's league at school. I had no business lusting after him outside of that fucked-up social world. Of course his parents were wealthy too. The only thing my dad was loaded with was vodka.

"This is my first season here. I had no idea. Sorry."

He reached out and touched my chin, lifting my gaze to his. "We need to talk." His brown eyes looked more serious than I'd ever seen them.

"I'm working, and we're slammed. My boss will flip his lid if I step away right now."

"What time do you get off?"

"I'll be here until close, around nine o'clock."

He nodded and brushed his thumb over my lower lip before his touch fell away. "Is anyone expecting you at home?"

I shook my head, keeping the truth sealed tight inside. My father was a waste of a human being now and wouldn't know if I was home or not. I could move out of state and it might take him months to notice.

"Good. I'll meet you by the swimming pool at nine thirty."

I nodded quickly, conflicting emotions whirling through me. I had no idea what Eric wanted to talk about, but I was about to find out.

ERIC

I spent the next hour ignoring my parents and younger brother. My focus was riveted on Clare's sexy little body wearing out the distance between the outside of the clubhouse and the bar inside. The older men at the bar were taking in eyefuls of her curvy ass whenever she walked away, and I wanted to slam their sloppy grins into their drinks.

Clare looked different. I couldn't figure it out. I'd shared the halls of Ridgeville High with her for four years. She'd been invisible to me, and now she was the only girl I could see. And I couldn't scrub out the memory of seeing her after her hookup with Travis.

If I'd had any doubts about what had gone on, they were swiftly removed when I talked to Travis about it. He had to go into all the details too. Her mouth was silk, and her tight pussy put Mandy's to shame. I cared less about him fucking my ex of several months than I did about him horning in on Clare. She was mine, and she was about to learn that lesson once and for all.

After the sun set, I made my way to the swimming pool to not-so-patiently wait for Clare. The air was cool and fragrant with summer. The course was quiet, save for a few stragglers heading to their cars after shifts at the restaurant. I shrouded myself in the darkness, a short distance from the edge of the illuminated pool. Several minutes later, she appeared. She looked around but didn't see me. With a heavy sigh, she dropped into a lounge chair, her head in her hands. I didn't envy her. My only job this summer was to stay in shape to start a new season in the fall.

After a moment she rose and looked around again. Not seeing me, she kicked off her shoes and set her apron, work shirt, and shorts on the lounge chair. In her bra and underwear, she dove into the pool. I tapped my foot, anxious to touch her. But I had to let her know I was serious before we got to the fun stuff. Then an idea hit me.

While she swam, I claimed her clothes and tucked them in a place she'd never find them. When I returned, she was swimming to the edge. She gasped when she saw me towering above her.

"Time to talk," I said.

She lifted herself from the pool and searched for her clothes to no avail. I tossed her a robe that I'd grabbed from the locker rooms.

"Come with me. I'll give you your clothes back after you've learned your lesson."

"What? I need those for work." Her voice was shrill with panic.

"Good. Then you'll be motivated to do as I say. Come with me."

Without waiting for her to answer, I walked toward the golf carts. Silently, she followed. I drove us far out onto the course, where no one would see us or hear us. I turned off the engine and sat silently a moment, revisiting my anger and all the things I wanted to say to Clare. The perfectly manicured greens were bathed in moonlight. When I glanced over at Clare, she was holding her robe tight to her chest.

"Tell me why you fucked Travis."

Her lips trembled. "I...I was having a bad day."

My teeth ground together. "Yeah, I was too after that. Believe it or not."

"I'm sorry. I didn't plan for you to see us."

"Is this the kind of girl you are now? Were you even a virgin when I fucked you?"

"Yes," she whispered.

Her eyes became glassy, and I immediately regretted my words. I was making her feel cheap. I knew she was a virgin. The feeling of breaking through her hymen was permanently etched in my mind, one of my all-time favorite memories actually. I had to take a different approach. I had to make her understand.

I stepped out of the cart and reached for her hand. She took it and stood before me.

"I know you were a virgin, Clare. And I understand you chose to share that part of yourself with me. I'll never, ever fucking forget it. The thing is, it's making me a little possessive knowing I was the first one to have you. And I don't feel like sharing you with every guy who gets a hard-on around you—which judging by the bar at the club, is a lot."

She shook her head vigorously. "I threw myself at Travis. I was desperate...for something. I don't know. But it wasn't his fault. I don't want you to blame him and ruin your friendship."

"Travis and I are fine. But if you want to spread your legs for another guy, you better make damn sure I never hear about it. Because if I do, I might kill him. Your pussy is mine, remember?"

Always will be. I heard the words in my head but caught them before they left my lips. This possessiveness I felt over her body was irrational.

She was breathing heavily, her eyes shifting over my expression like she was trying to read me. I unfastened her robe, slid the belt from it, and pushed the garment from her shoulders. I caught her hands in mine, kissed her palms, and sucked her fingertips. Then I wound the belt around her wrists, binding her tightly.

"What are you doing?" Her voice was shaky, from fear or desire, I couldn't know for sure.

"I'm teaching you a lesson, Clare. You do everything I tell you, and you'll get your things back. If we disagree, chances are high that I'll leave you out here to find your way back, and you'll never see your work clothes again. Understand?"

"Yes," she whispered.

I wanted her to show me, not tell me.

"Travis tells me great things about your mouth. I want to see if we can do things with it that he hasn't. Get on your knees, Clare."

CLARE

I was shaking from head to toe, but the second he wound the robe belt around my wrists, my pussy became incredibly wet. I wasn't sure what Eric was capable of, but I also desperately wanted to find out. I'd never seen this dominant side of him. He'd seemed so fun-loving at school, a picture-perfect guy with an easy demeanor. He was intense on the field, of course. But I couldn't quite fathom seeing that passion directed at me...of all people.

I dropped to my knees and worked his fly open as best I could. His cock was so hard it nearly hit me in the face when I freed him from his boxer shorts. I wasted no time in latching my mouth around him. I breathed him in, moaning when his flavor settled over my tongue. God help me, I loved Eric Hayward, and I loved his cock.

I rubbed my thighs together, trying to ease the ache between them, all the while working his length into my mouth, taking as much of him as I could. Eric gazed down at me, like he was taking a video with his mind. I had no idea how I was measuring up to the other girls who'd given him blowjobs.

"That's a good girl. You suck my cock so good. Here..."

When he took his cock out of my mouth and lifted it, presenting his balls to me, I wasted no time in giving them a tongue bath. I sucked each one into my mouth, releasing it with a pop when I let go. He groaned and sighed, and I had a feeling I was doing a pretty good job. Already I'd done a lot more than I had with Travis. As much as I enjoyed Eric's pleasure though, I really wanted some of my own. The ache in my pussy was almost painful at this point.

Before I could beg him for a release, he put his cock back in my mouth, and after a few deep strokes, a shot of warm liquid coated my throat. He'd come. Goddamn him. I swallowed down his release, taking note of his unique flavor as I wrestled with my emotions.

I felt like an angry toddler in a store. *I* wanted to come too.

He sighed again, zipped up his pants, and walked a lazy circle around the twelfth hole. He stretched his arms into the air and contemplated the full moon for a moment before returning to me.

"I'll be back in a bit. I need to take care of something."

"What? You can't leave me out here."

He leaned down and grasped my jaw. "I can and I will. And you're not going to argue with me about it, are you, Clare?"

"Eric, please."

"Head down and ass in the air. You better be that way for me when I get back, or you'll regret it."

But before I could argue with his preposterous request, he jumped onto the cart and drove out of sight.

I was alone and naked. Horny beyond hope and completely at the mercy of the only boy I'd ever really loved. I groaned and pounded my bound fists on the cushioned turf. I rested my head on the robe under me and sighed. Did I love Eric? Did he deserve my love? I tried to remember his sweetness over this new angry side of him. As I did, I melted into the ground and took my pose, praying that no one could see me in this compromising position.

Many minutes passed before I heard the sound of a cart engine again. My heart raced, and I resisted the urge to look up. It had to be Eric. No one else would be here, right here, at this hour. Still, if it were anyone else, I'd be fired—not to mention completely humiliated.

The engine cut, and I heard quiet footfalls on the grass.

"You are a good girl, aren't you? Have you always been that way?"

I nodded slightly, relieved at the sound of Eric's voice.

"Talk to me."

I swallowed over the emotion thick in my throat. "I've always tried to be good. To follow the rules and hope that people will like me and that one day, I'll find myself in a better place."

"Has it worked?"

"Sometimes. Sometimes not being good is better. Depends on the day."

He knelt behind me and slid his fingers through my wet folds. "You can be bad with me, Clare. But only with me. I need to know this cunt is mine."

He shoved his fingers deep into me. A sound—part gasp, part feral cry—left my lips. I needed that. Oh, I needed that. Then he withdrew, and I groaned in frustration.

"Promise me," he said softly.

"I promise, Eric. I'll be good, unless I can be bad with you. But you have to make me a promise too."

"You're not in a position to be making demands."

"If you ruin me like this, out here, I'll lose my job. I may not be able to support myself next year at school. My family isn't like yours. I'm not making demands. I'm asking you to give me something in return for what I'll give to you."

He was silent and brought his touch back to my aching sex, a gentle teasing stroke that I hoped meant he would at least hear me out.

"Eric, promise me that if I give myself to you, and only you, that you'll take care of my needs. You can't give girls like Mandy the piece of you that I want and ignore me for weeks or months on end. You showed me what sex could be like, and now I want it. I crave it. And I crave it with you more than anyone else, I swear it."

He began rubbing me steadily, and a fiery heat licked over my skin.

"So you want attention, sweet Clare? Okay, I can give you attention. In exchange for exclusive access to your pussy."

"Thank you." I pushed my hips back into his touch, desperate for the release that was just under the surface.

God, I wish he hadn't come already. I wanted his cock in me, pounding me savagely. But this sensation was different. I had been able to bring myself to orgasm this way a few times but always felt kind of ridiculous. Being bent over in the middle of a golf course with Eric's fingers defiling me felt far less ridiculous. It felt delicious and decadent and bad.

And I had told him the truth. Being bad didn't just feel good—it felt amazing when I was with him.

Mercifully, he slipped back into my pussy, two fingers and then three, and used his other hand to pinch and stimulate my swollen clit. I rocked into him and moaned against the robe. I was climbing, closer...so fucking close.

"Scream for me. Every time you come for me, I don't want you holding anything back. I don't care where we are or who hears. Fucking come for me now, Clare. Now!"

I twisted my fingers into the terry cloth and let the orgasm rip through me with a scream, not caring who heard me or how vulnerable I was in front of him. The sensation piqued and then slowly melted away. With it, I sank to the ground, exhausted from my release. Moisture collected at the edges of my eyes, and I struggled to catch my breath.

In that moment, nothing could have been more achingly clear. My body belonged to Eric Hayward.

CHAPTER FOUR

CLARE

The warm tropical sun felt heavenly against my skin. We'd only been on the island of Kauai for a day, and I was already sporting a nice golden tan. My best friend Megan hadn't been so fortunate. She was nursing a mild case of sunburn beneath a large beach umbrella beside me.

I adjusted my ear buds and rolled over onto my stomach when my iPod shuffled to play one of my new favorite songs. I was happily humming along with the chorus when something very cold and wet hit my ass.

"What the—" I jerked the ear buds from my ears and flipped over onto my side, catching a glimpse of the culprit lying on the sand next to me—a canary-yellow Frisbee.

Megan shot up in her lounger and grabbed my arm. "Holy. Fuck. Me. There is a god on the beach." She slid her sunglasses down to the end of her nose.

Chuckling, I shook my head at her dramatics. From the moment we'd stepped off the plane, the girl had been on the prowl for the ultimate Hawaiian hookup, like it was number one on her bucket list. We'd spent most of our day yesterday sunning in this exact same spot, rating men as they walked up and down the beach. I'd joined in on the fun just to appease her, but so far I hadn't been that impressed. Most of the guys I'd seen failed miserably in comparison to Eric.

That was until my gaze landed on the gorgeous blond beach god himself.

Bringing a hand up to shield my eyes, I fixed my gaze on the glorious six feet of perfection stepping out of the ocean. The bright afternoon sun made his shoulder-length hair glow against his tanned body, which was dripping wet and glistening from head to toe. Watching him was like seeing my most sinful fantasy play out right in front of me; something I had plenty of experience with lately.

Biting down on my lower lip, I drank him in, slowly, appreciating every inch of his ripped body like he was a piece of rare artwork. Just as I dared a look down to the perfect V that dipped below the waistband of his red board shorts, Megan snapped me from my dirty thoughts.

"Shit! He's coming this way," she said in a hushed voice.

The hot surfer approached. His impressive shadow completely blocked the sun. Goddamn. Even his shadow was smoking hot.

"Hey," he said, flashing me a smile so sexy it should have been illegal. He rubbed the back of his neck with his hand and shifted his stance in the sand before eyeing the Frisbee in my hand. "I'm really sorry you got hit. I swear that gust of wind came out of nowhere."

"Oh, it's totally fine. Really. There's no need to apologize."

As I handed it back to him, his fingertips lightly brushed against my hand. The exchange electrified me. When I looked up at him, his wide-eyed expression mirrored my own. *Get a hold of yourself, Clare.*

He extended his hand out to me again. "Reed Michaels."

"Clare Winston," I replied, taking it.

"Clare," he repeated, rewarding me again with his deadly smile. The sexy way my name resonated from his lips gave me goose bumps.

"And, I'm Megan," my best friend chimed in from beside me, her voice coming off with a purr.

His glance met hers but quickly returned to me. "Listen, my friend and I scored some VIP tickets to this new club that just opened on the island. Would you two like to join us tomorrow night?"

I hesitated with my answer, struggling to find a polite way to decline his invitation. After all, I had Eric back at home. We'd finally come to an understanding. As much as I wanted to go to the club, I didn't want to do anything that might jeopardize things with our relationship.

"We'd love to," Megan answered before I could speak.

I shot her a murderous look, but she was too busy drooling over Reed to even notice.

"Great." He beamed and turned around to wave his friend over to us.

My attention was immediately drawn to the large colorful tattoo of a flaming tidal wave that stretched, shoulder to shoulder, across Reed's muscular back. The blues and vibrant orange captivated me. I admired the incredible detail. *Beautiful.* I'd never seen anything like it. But then again, I'd never seen anything like him before either.

"Clare, Megan, this is my buddy, Cole." Reed introduced us to his handsome friend.

I glanced over at Megan. *Yep, she is definitely giving Cole a high rating in her head.*

"Are you two staying here?" Reed motioned toward the beachside hotel sprawling behind us.

"Yes, we're here until Monday," Megan added.

I narrowed my eyes at her.

"Well then, it's settled. Cole and I will meet you in the hotel lobby tomorrow around eight."

Bracing himself on the arms of my chair, Reed leaned down over me. He looked into my eyes at a distance so close, I felt as though my breath was being sucked from my chest.

Fuck. Me.

I fluttered my eyelids at him, instantly drunk on the sexual energy that was seeping from our bodies.

The sides of Reed's mouth turned up into a grin, as if he had somehow heard every conflicting thought swirling in my head.

"Don't stand me up, Clare, or I'll have to come up and fetch you. Come to think of it, that might be fun." He winked.

Breathless, I admired his perfectly tanned physique as he ran back toward the water.

Reed Michaels was a dangerous temptation.

Exciting.

Sexy.

Completely off limits.

And, I already wanted him like there was no tomorrow.

ERIC

"Yes!"

I fist-bumped Travis as we proudly celebrated our beer pong victory. We were undoubtedly wasted, but still more sober than our opponents—which wasn't saying a lot. No doubt about it. Tomorrow's hangover was going to suck. But, right now, I wasn't concerned about that. The night was still young, and the beer keg was still flowing.

"Drink! Drink! Drink!"

I started the chant, and soon my teammates joined in. Smiling, I threw my arm around my best friend's shoulders and watched the losing team chug their beers. Once they were done, empty plastic cups went flying in the air.

In keeping with Ridgeville tradition, the senior football players were throwing a party at Coach Parton's lake house. Since Clare was away on her trip, I more than welcomed the distraction. She'd only been gone a few days, but I already had a serious case of blue balls. I was counting down the days until I could sink my cock back into her sweet pussy again. Clare had no goddamn idea how addicted I was to her or our late nights at the country club. We'd christened every hole on the course...

I'd been with more than my share of girls, but Clare was different. The best part was...now she was all mine.

A set of headlights turned into the driveway, illuminating the back yard.

"Girls are here!" Travis announced, winking in my direction.

Glancing back toward the vehicle, I cursed. The horny son of a bitch had planned all of this without telling me. I should have known he'd pull something.

Whistles and catcalls erupted as the group approached, girls from school, most wearing skimpy bikini tops and barely-there cut-off shorts. When I saw Mandy glance in my direction, my blood began to boil.

I didn't want her anywhere near me. And I knew I needed to remove myself from temptation. The last thing I wanted was the alcohol in my system to drive me to do something I would regret later.

Deciding to call it a night, I staggered across the lawn and through the dark house in search of my room. I barely made it to the end of the bed before I collapsed onto the mattress. The image of Clare's beautiful face was the last thing I remembered before I gave in to my drunken haze.

◆ ◆ ◆ ◆

I awoke to a familiar moan in my ear. When I opened my eyes, Mandy filled my frame of vision. Throwing back the covers, I leapt from the bed, narrowly avoiding tripping over my own feet.

"What the hell are you doing in here?" I jerked my shorts up off the floor and dressed quickly.

"It's where you wanted me, don't you remember?" Mandy pouted her lips and rolled over to her back.

I looked down at her naked body and panicked.

"Wait a minute. We didn't, did we?" I was terrified to know the truth.

She smirked, holding a ripped condom wrapper between her fingers. "Several times, actually."

My stomach dropped. "No, no, no!"

Frantic, I shoved my hands into my hair, pulling hard at the ends.

Think, Eric. Think. What happened last night?

"I must say, your stamina has certainly improved. I had a hard time keeping up." She licked her lips, rose off the bed, and walked toward me, obviously proud of her nakedness. "I'm more than ready for another round," she purred, tracing her fingers down my bare chest.

I shoved her hand away and brushed past her. "Fuck!" I patted my pockets for my phone. "Where's my fucking phone, Mandy?"

Amusement played at her lips as she sat on the edge of the bed, crossed her long legs, and watched me search the room. "It's probably in the bed somewhere. You got a little creative with it last night."

Goddamn it. Can this possibly get any worse?

Tearing the bedding from the mattress, I found my phone tangled among the tan sheets. Scrolling through my notifications, I noticed Mandy had sent me a video from her phone.

"What the hell is this?" Dread dropped like a stone in my gut.

"I thought you might want a little reminder from last night."

"Have you lost your mind? Who else have you sent this to?"

She smirked. "A few people. Just the ones I knew would like to watch."

"Did you send this to Clare?" I snarled.

She shrugged. "Maybe."

The panic and dread morphed into a heavy guilt. I dropped to the edge of the bed, bracing my elbows on my knees as I held my head in my hands. "Oh, my God. What have I done?"

Mandy climbed behind me on the bed and massaged my tense shoulders.

"She can't satisfy you, Eric. Last night just proved that. I gave you what you wanted, what you needed...and you loved it."

I jumped to my feet. "Get your goddamn hands off me, Mandy. I was drunk. I didn't know what I was doing."

She narrowed her eyes. "Don't give me that shit, Eric. You weren't that wasted. You knew exactly what you were doing."

Her words seemed to be stuck on repeat in my head.

You knew exactly what you were doing.

Throwing my shirt over my head, I bolted toward the door.

"Where are you going?" she snapped, the anger in her voice undeniable.

"I'm going to fix this."

"Come on, Eric. She's never going to forgive you."

"Maybe not. But I'll be damned if I'm going to lose her."

CLARE

The intoxicating aromas of bodies and sex permeated the febrile air of the busy nightclub. As I moved my body to the beat of the music, I became increasingly aware of just how close I was dancing to Reed. Our bodies moved back and forth in perfect sync, as if we'd always been familiar with one another. Earlier, when he had pulled me onto the dance floor, I'd convinced myself that dancing with him was harmless. But the instant his hands were on my hips, I knew I was heading straight into dangerous territory. The scary part was...I wanted it.

A bead of sweat trickled down my neck. As if he had read my mind, Reed lifted up my long strawberry curls and blew against my nape. The delicious sensation took a direct path to my pussy, which was already begging for release.

Once the song ended, I took his hand and led him toward the bar to cool off. I knew if I spent another five minutes on that dance floor with him, there would be no way I'd be able to keep my promise to Eric. I had grown to care for him far too much over the past month to jeopardize anything by indulging in a hot paradise fling with Reed— not that I hadn't entertained the idea thoroughly in my head at least a few dozen times since this afternoon.

Fanning myself, I climbed onto one of the barstools. Reed looked like perfect sin in his form-fitting black shirt and dark denim jeans. But the best part was the man bun he was sporting. With his long blond hair pulled away from his face, he looked even more breathtaking. I felt like every woman in here had already eye-fucked him at least once.

"You're a great dancer," Reed shouted over the club music while waving the bartender over to us.

"Thanks, you're not so bad yourself."

The bartender sat two bottles of cold water in front of us and then patted his hand on the bar to get Reed's attention.

"Good luck on Saturday, bro. My buddies and I will be rooting for you."

Reed shook his hand. "Thanks, man. I really appreciate that."

He handed me a water and I lifted my brow, eyeing him curiously as I twisted the cap off the bottle. "What's Saturday?"

"The Sterling Beach Classic. The top five surfers will be eligible for the World Cup next month in Sydney."

"Wow, so you're a pro surfer? That's awesome!"

Reed reached down and took my hand in his. He studied our entwined fingers for a minute before lifting his eyes to mine. "I know you're dating someone, but I would really love it if you could be there Saturday. After the rough preliminary round last week, I could definitely use a good luck charm." His dark eyes looked hopeful as he waited for my answer.

Oh, come on, Clare. What could it hurt?

I relaxed my shoulders and softened my expression. "Sure, I'd love to come."

Like I'd pass up a chance to see the ocean god wet and shirtless again.

Reed placed a tender kiss on my hand, sending my pounding clit into overdrive. Jesus, the man was going to make me come apart in the middle of this club.

My phone unexpectedly vibrated in the bodice of my dress, causing me to jump.

A message came in from an unknown number. The text instantly grabbed my attention.

When the cat's away, the mouse will play.

What the hell did that mean? Then another message came through with a video attached. Something told me not to open it, but I couldn't stop myself.

I excused myself to the ladies room. After securing the door to the stall, I hurriedly retrieved my phone from the top part of my dress. My thumb hovered over the play triangle for a few more seconds before I was brave enough to continue. The second my gaze landed on the figures moving on the screen, I wished I had listened to the voice in my head.

I couldn't hear the audio over the loud club music thumping outside the bathroom, but I didn't need to. The vivid image of Mandy's naked body bouncing up and down over the midsection of a guy told me everything. My hands shook as the angle of the video shifted, revealing another girl. She was sitting on the face of the guy, rocking back and forth as he ate her eagerly.

Suddenly, Mandy's scream overpowered the noisy club. "Eric!"

I powered off my phone with trembling hands. Disoriented, I stumbled out of the bathroom stall and gripped the sides of the counter to keep my legs from going out beneath me. *How could he do this to me?*

I gave myself a few minutes to recover and decided I had to move. I opened the door, shocked to see Reed leaning against the adjacent wall. The broad smile on his handsome face dropped the instant his eyes landed on me. In one quick move, he was in front of me, both arms wrapped firmly around me.

"Clare? What's wrong? Are you okay?" His voice was full of concern.

I buried my head into his chest. "H-He cheated on me, Reed. Someone sent me a video of him in bed with two girls. How could he be so cruel?"

He cursed under his breath before saying, "Come on. Let's get you out of here." He tightened his grip around my waist and led me down the hallway.

♦ ♦ ♦ ♦

Reed's Jeep had barely stopped in the vacant beach parking lot before I opened the passenger side door.

"Clare!" He grabbed for my arm, but I pulled away. "Clare, wait!" Reed shouted from behind me.

Quickly, I kicked off my heels and took off toward the ocean.

Images of Mandy riding Eric flashed before my eyes, sending

a sharp pain through me. I ran until my chest was burning, until I couldn't breathe. Gasping for air, I stumbled in the sand. Within seconds, Reed was by my side, kneeling next to me.

"How could I have been so stupid?"

In one gentle movement, I was sitting in Reed's lap, my head against his chest, breathing him in as he held me against him. God, he smelled so fucking good.

Gently, using the pad of his thumb, Reed wiped at a single tear that fell down my cheek. "He's not worth a single one of these, Clare. You need to forget about him."

"I want to forget." I tightened my grip on the front of Reed's shirt, pulling him to me until his mouth was inches from mine. "Please, Reed, make me forget," I whispered against his lips, begging for him to do something, anything to take the pain away.

"Clare." His voice was strained.

Desperate to feel him, I began frantically working to unfasten his pants. I'd barely managed to loosen his belt buckle before Reed's strong hands seized my wrists, forcefully pushing me backward until my back hit the sand.

Pinning my hands above me, he leaned over me, a pained look on his face. "Stop."

I immediately stilled at his words. *Stop?* My face heated with embarrassment. He was rejecting me. I turned my head, too mortified to look at him.

"I-I'm sorry. I thought you wanted me."

Using his knee to urge my legs apart, Reed slid one hand beneath my ass and then tugged me toward him until his hardness was flush against my heated opening. I gasped at the delectable sensation.

"Does that fucking feel like I don't want you?"

Reed rotated his hips, grinding his pelvis against my swollen clit, but then suddenly stilled, tracing his thumb across my trembling bottom lip. Unable to speak, I stared back at him through lustful eyes.

"You have no idea how badly I want to rip that dress off you and fuck you until you forget your own name."

I whimpered, wanting more, needing more. "What's stopping you then? Take me, Reed. Please."

Reed tensed, pressing his forehead to mine.

"No, Clare. Not this way. You can't fuck someone out of your head. You need someone to appreciate your body, to make love to you."

He slowly inched his hand up my thigh.

"Tell me. Has anyone ever taken their time with you?" He placed a gentle kiss against my neck, licking down to the crevice of my chest. My body arched against the sand.

"No," I breathed, my voice trembling.

He brushed his lips across my bottom lip. "Then maybe it's time someone did."

ERIC

"Come on, Clare. Please, pick up."

I had been blowing up her phone nonstop with calls and texts for the past hour, hoping and praying that by some miracle she'd answer. Her voicemail was already maxed out with my lengthy apologies. Reaching the point of desperation, I'd even resorted to tracking down Megan's cell phone number. She was also ignoring my calls. No surprise there.

The screen door creaked as Travis stepped onto the front porch. He shot me a sympathetic look before sitting in the rocking chair beside me. Everyone else had already left the lake house.

"Still not answering, huh?"

Frustrated, I ran my hand through my hair. "I fucked up bad, and I don't know how in the hell to make it right."

Travis cleared his throat. "Look, I didn't want to say anything while the girls were still here, but I overheard a conversation in the kitchen that makes me think that Mandy's up to something."

I rolled my eyes. "When isn't she up to something?"

He held out his hand. "Let me see that video again."

Cringing, I handed my phone to him.

"When you're done, delete it. I want it off my phone."

As he watched, I sat back in the rocker, becoming nauseous as the sounds of Mandy's moaning permeated my ears.

How could I have been so fucking stupid?

"That bitch!" Travis scooted to the edge of his seat. "She set you up, bro."

He turned the phone around for me to see the paused image on the screen. My focus zeroed in on the hand that was gripping Mandy's ass. The familiar brown leather cuff around the wrist gave it all away.

"Peyton? Are you fucking kidding me? But I thought he couldn't make it."

Travis shook his head. "He showed up late last night, but didn't stay long. He was pissed when he left. Now it all makes sense."

A sense of relief washed over me, but it was short lived. Even though I was innocent, the damage had already been done. I had just a couple more days before Clare returned from Hawaii. If I had any hope of making this right between us, I would have to come up with one hell of a plan. One thing was for sure. I wasn't going to lose her.

CLARE

We left the beach and were at Reed's apartment, in his bedroom, shrouded in darkness. Reed tugged down the side zipper of my dress and slowly eased it off my body. I stood in front of him, wearing only a white lace thong. So many emotions swirled through me, but in this moment, I felt beautiful...appreciated...cherished even.

With a hunger in his eyes that stole my breath, he slowly slid his palms up my sides, over my arms, before cradling my face. Lowering his forehead to mine, our lips a breath apart, he growled with need. I opened for him, ready for his kiss. But before our lips touched, he swooped his arms under my knees and carried me back into his bedroom.

A second later, he eased me against the silky bedding. I lifted my hips as he gripped the sides of my thong, dragged the lacy fabric down my legs, and tossed them to the side.

"No one should ever rush being with you, Clare." He gently kissed right above my mound before sliding his hands between my legs, easing them apart. "You should be treasured." Keeping his eyes on mine, he swiped his searing hot tongue across the lips of my pussy. "You should be savored. Worshipped."

Prowling above me, Reed licked a long trail up my abdomen, pausing to flick his tongue against my erect nipple. A mischievous look spread across his face as he pursed his lips and blew across the wetness. I arched up off the bed, every inch of my body humming with pleasure.

When I opened my eyes, he leaned in over me, brushing my curls back away from my face.

"So fucking beautiful," he whispered against my lips before covering my mouth with his.

I moaned in delight, tasting the flavor of cinnamon on his tongue. *God, could he kiss!*

Every delectable swipe of his tongue against mine felt like I was falling, deeper and deeper, into a blissful euphoria. I was so deliciously lost in him. If kissing him was this incredible, I couldn't begin to fathom how amazing sex would be.

Taking his time, Reed feathered kisses over every inch of my body. When he hungrily engulfed my breast, I cried out in pleasure. Reed's appreciative groans only turned me on more. If he kept this up, I was going to come.

I almost whimpered with relief at the sound of the condom wrapper ripping. Then he wrapped his arms around my bare waist and lifted me up so I was straddling him. I felt his long, hard cock twitch beneath me, teasing me and triggering the heaviness in my core to bear down, hard. My pussy ached to be filled. I didn't know how much more I could stand. Every kiss, every touch was only making me more desperate.

He slid his palms beneath my ass to support me while he aligned the tip of his sheathed cock to my soaked opening.

"Slow," he reminded me with a raspy breath.

I obeyed, savoring every inch of progress. I trembled at the feel of his thick girth stretching me, filling me. Reed covered my mouth with his, groaning when I seated him fully. Overwhelmed with pleasure, I closed my eyes, dropped my head back, and rotated my hips.

"Eyes on me, Clare," he demanded gently. "I want you to see what you do to me."

In perfect sync we moved together, slowly, taking our time to relish each thrust.

With our gazes locked, my climb to release rose sharply. It was as if every single movement he made was connected to my inner core.

"Reed. Oh, God...you feel so good."

"Let go, baby. Come."

I let the feelings take me under. As a powerful orgasm rippled through me, Reed captured my face, quickening his pace, until I felt my pleasure soak his cock.

Before I could catch my breath, Reed eased me onto my back. He remained thick and swollen inside me, thrusting deeper. I moaned, wrapping my legs around his waist.

Reed pressed his forehead to mine, with his legs pressed beneath my thighs until my knees rested against my chest. I gasped at how deliciously deep he was.

"You feel like heaven. So." *Thrust.* "Fucking." *Thrust.* "Perfect." *Thrust.*

His powerful words were my undoing, triggering the most explosive orgasm I'd ever experienced.

"See what you do to me?" He panted, his strides growing more powerful. "Oh, God, Clare. I'm going to come."

I studied his face intently as he chased his pleasure, his mouth gaping open as he shuddered above me. Watching him come had been the most beautifully erotic thing I'd ever seen.

Panting, he tenderly kissed my lips before easing out of me. I grieved the absence of his cock, my swollen sex still craving him.

Nestling against him, I rested my head against his chest and tried to catch my breath.

"That was... Wow." He tightened his embrace, rubbing my arms tenderly. I raised my head, smiling adoringly at his handsome face.

He stared into my eyes and played with one of my long curls. "I can't tell you how incredible that was, Clare. Nothing has ever felt as good as you."

I blushed at his compliment.

Chuckling, he kissed the tip of my nose. "I didn't mean to embarrass you."

"I just didn't know sex could be like this. It was so perfect."

He was silent a moment, studying me before speaking. "No one should take you for granted, Clare. Promise me you won't forget that."

I nodded, dropping my head so that he wouldn't see the tears in my eyes. This man was unbelievable. Was he really a god?

Reed tilted my chin up with his fingertips, a sly grin forming at his lips.

"I think maybe I need to make damn sure you never forget."

I barely had time to register what he'd said before he moved back between my legs.

Reed Michaels was a determined man, making his point three more times that night.

ERIC

"What time does her plane get in tomorrow?" Travis carried the last case of beer from the back of his dad's bar. I popped a handful of nuts in my mouth, wishing that I could wash them down with one of the cold beers he'd just put in the cooler.

"Nine o'clock tonight. Hopefully it won't be delayed."

Smirking, he leaned over the bar. "So you're really going to risk making a spectacle of yourself in front of everyone over a girl?"

"Not *a* girl, *my* girl." I corrected. When it came to earning back Clare Winston, I was willing to undergo any form of public humiliation—even if that meant that the FAA ended up banning me permanently from the airport.

"Well, when you get hauled into a room and cavity searched, don't say I didn't warn you."

Travis's attention shifted to something behind me. Lifting up his arm, he pointed toward the huge television hanging on the wall.

"Holy shit! Isn't that Clare?"

Clare? Why the hell would she be on ESPN?

"Turn it up!" I shouted, practically leaping for the remote on the bar.

"We're coming at you live from the beautiful island of Kauai where Reed Michaels has just won the Sterling Beach Classic. Reed, congratulations on your win. Some here are calling that cutback move on that last wave a gutsy decision. That's definitely something we've not seen from you this season. Can you tell us what motivated you to change it up?"

I grimaced as the blond surfer snaked his arm around Clare's waist, tugging her close to him. Immediately, I wanted to rip his goddamn arm off his body. Without wavering, the surfer kept his focus on Clare as he answered.

"This beautiful girl coming into my life is what motivated me." Then, he pulled her in for a kiss.

It took everything in me to fight back the urge to break every fucking bottle in the place. Travis quickly hit the button on the remote to change the channel, as if that was going to alleviate the situation.

I hadn't missed the way Clare had looked at him. It was the same way she used to look at me when she was still mine.

Mine.

"That doesn't mean anything, Eric." Travis tried to console me, but it was pointless.

"Yes, it does. It means I've lost her."

"No, it doesn't. Grow some fucking balls, Eric, and go get your girl."

CLARE

Reed held my hand as we walked through the crowded airport. I told him last night that he didn't have to come, but he insisted on seeing us off. Megan and Cole had already said their goodbyes, leaving the two of us alone.

Reed wrapped his arms around my waist and pulled me against him. I stared into his dark eyes, wishing I could stay longer.

"I have a confession to make," he said, smirking.

"Okay, let's have it."

"That day on the beach with the Frisbee? Well, let's just say my aim was spot-on."

I busted out laughing. "You're something else, you know it?"

Reed's expression suddenly grew serious. "I know your heart still belongs with him." He cupped my face with his hands. "But you've stolen mine, Clare Winston." He tenderly kissed me, and then dragged his bottom lip in to savor it.

"I'll never forget you, Reed. You've made me feel so special."

"You *are* special, my beautiful girl. Never forget that."

When the boarding call for my flight was announced, I struggled to let go of him. He lifted me up, giving me one final passionate kiss before setting me down.

Drunk on the kiss, I fluttered my eyes open.

"This isn't goodbye, Clare. I'll see you again."

◆ ◆ ◆ ◆

Megan snored lightly next to me on the plane. I was grateful for the peace. It gave me time to process everything in my head without her prying questions. I knew she wanted details about my time with Reed, but I wasn't sure I wanted to give them to her. I wanted to keep them safely tucked away, to remind me how special sex could be between two people.

Resting my head against the window, I stared out at the evening sky. Reed had been right. My heart still completely belonged to Eric. Being with Reed only solidified that I deserved more than what Eric had given me. Sure, I'd loved our time together, but Reed had also opened my eyes up to how incredible slow, tender love could be. More than anything, I wanted to experience that with Eric, except I didn't know where we stood. Could I forgive him?

I was completely exhausted by the time our plane landed. All I wanted to do was go home, crawl into bed, and sleep. Dropping my head, I followed my best friend off the plane. When I looked up, I saw the very last person I expected to see standing in the middle of the airport. My heart stopped at the sight of Eric.

Holding an armful of flowers, he moved toward me. "It was all a lie, Clare. That wasn't me in the video. She set it up to keep us apart. I swear. Just give me a chance, and I can prove it to you."

"Eric." I said his name on a whispered breath.

He stepped closer, tipping my face up until I was gazing into his eyes. "I didn't sleep with her. I'd never—"

"But, Eric. It's not that simple. I..." I swallowed hard. I needed to be honest about everything that had happened with Reed. But how could I tell him if what he said was really true?

Eric interrupted me by pressing his finger to my lips. "Shhh. I don't care what happened in Hawaii. It's in the past. You and me? We're the future."

CHAPTER FIVE

CLARE

The last few weeks of summer passed in a blur. Shifts at work filled my days, and secret rendezvous with Eric filled my nights. He more than met my physical needs. He defined them. He was the captain of my pleasure, and I was nothing short of addicted to the intimacy we shared.

Though we hadn't planned it intentionally, both Eric and I had been admitted to the same university. When the time came to pack up and leave behind life in Ridgeville, we promised to pick things back up once we got settled into our dorms and learned our schedules.

For all those promises, I wasn't prepared for three weeks of near silence. If we hadn't been at the same college, I might have expected it—maybe—but we weren't that far from each other. Still, the campus was enormous and we shared it with tens of thousands of other students from all over the country.

Eric was a freshman, but a well-positioned one. I had come into my own over the summer, but my uncertainties crept in. I was nobody in Ridgeville. Could I expect to be someone different here?

Eric had answered a few texts, but he was busy with an intense training schedule and, of course, classes. Maybe I should have given him the benefit of the doubt. But without his cock regularly inside me, reassuring me that he cared about me and our relationship, my insecurities were raging.

By the third weekend, I caved and invited Megan to come visit me. She was attending a private college only a short bus ride away. When she arrived on Saturday, we spent the afternoon drinking her new favorite—boxed wine—and choosing outfits for a night out. We were going to prowl campus parties until we couldn't stand, which would be more fun than working ahead on my Psych assignments.

I tried on a tight black tube top that Megan had brought and assessed myself in the mirror. Not me. Not at all.

"I love it!" Megan announced loudly, nearly spilling a paper cup of wine on her satiny red halter top.

"I can't pull this off."

"Are you kidding me? You need to get over this shy shit, Clare. You're in college and you're a ten."

I rolled my eyes. "No one seems to think that about me."

"Because you're not showing off your assets, girl."

I shrugged and turned side to side, reconsidering the choice. I riffled through my drawers and found some skinny jeans that I'd bought but never had the guts to wear. The outfit came together, but disappointment and doubt kept welling up. I thought about calling Eric and seeing what he was up to, but then I imagined him blowing me off, which would only ruin my night.

I flopped on the beige carpet and filled a fresh cup to the brim. Megan put her hand on mine when I finished it. "What's on your mind, Clare? Do you like it here?"

I sighed. "I do and I don't. The classes are great, really challenging..."

Megan groaned and rolled her eyes. "Clare, I do not care about how challenging the core curriculum is. I want to know about you." She poked her finger where my heart beat under my ribcage. "What is going on with Clare?"

"I guess I'm lonely." I shrugged. "I miss you, and even though I've made a few friends, no one compares. And I haven't really met any guys. I thought college would be different."

"College *is* different. So *you* should be too. This is our chance to start over, Clare. We're not the book nerds and theater geeks we were at Ridgeville. We can be whoever we want to be. Especially at a school this big. Rock your skank clothes, and let's act like we're in college. Fuck the baggage and fuck the people we used to be."

I inhaled a deep breath, pulling all of her kind wisdom in with it. When I exhaled, I imagined exhaling the old Clare. The one who never felt good enough. The one who woke up every morning wondering if Eric had texted her, like he was the only thing in life that mattered. Pathetic. Megan was right. I needed to get it together and take charge of my life, with or without Eric.

Full of renewed determination, I raised my glass with a toast. "You are completely fucking right, as usual."

ERIC

The music pounded loudly, vibrating the walls of the shabby frat house living room and my eardrums. The house was packed, thick with smoke and the crush of college kids partying. Drinking, laughing, kissing, shouting.

I welcomed the chaos, the blur of strangers in a strange place that was slowly becoming home. College was a rush of newness, one experience stacked right up on the next. It was busy, intense, intimidating, thrilling, and oddly lacking. I missed Clare, but still I couldn't bring myself to arrange a time to meet her. Truth was I'd already scoped out her dorm. I could drop in on her anytime, kiss her, feel her velvety skin, have her, and fall into those scary emotions I felt whenever she was near.

But I hadn't. Instead, I'd watched her like a fucking stalker. She went to class with friends and came back again. There was only one guy in her group, and though he looked innocent enough, I had to restrain myself from intervening whenever I saw her with him. Because she deserved freedom. Experiences. A chance to be the woman she was meant to be. Without Mandy and all the other people at Ridgeville who'd always looked down on her. She could be someone new here. Sure, she could be the girlfriend of the freshman quarterback, and I'd be proud to give her that title, but there was so much more to life than being the girl on my arm. She was too smart, too pure, too good to get wrapped up in that stupidity.

I couldn't stake my claim over her, demanding her pussy and her heart for myself. Every cell of my being wanted to...but somewhere inside my self-serving heart, I wanted more for her. I had to give her space to be her own person. Even if it was tearing me up inside.

A curvy girl bounced down on my lap, breaking me from my familiar cycle of troubling thoughts. I saw her tits before I saw her face. Nice and round, benefiting from the serious padding of the lacy bra that was peeking out from under her tank top.

"I'm Daisy." She held out her hand to me, and I shook it wordlessly. "You're Eric Hayward. Number twelve, right?"

She shifted on my lap, a motion that was probably supposed to seem casual but she was basically rubbing her pussy on my thigh. I was too defeated missing Clare to really care. I nodded and took a sip of my beer.

"I bet you get a lot of girls who know who you are, don't you?"

I finally glanced up at her. She had light blond hair pulled into a tight ponytail that curled over her shoulder. She was pretty, but she wasn't Clare. She was also one hundred percent right.

"You've got that right," I finally said.

She cocked her head and put her finger on the wrinkle between my eyebrows. "You look like you need to have a little fun, Mr. Hayward."

I nodded again absently. She might be right, but I just wanted to get drunk on this piss-odor couch, fall into my room, and dream of Clare. I closed my eyes. Her pretty little tits. Her sweet cunt. Wild curls that kissed her shoulders and fell down her back when she was arching and bowing under an orgasm that I was giving her. I exhaled and felt a hand stroking my growing erection.

I opened my eyes. Daisy had sex written all over her features. Supple glossy lips and half-lidded eyes. God, if only she was my beautiful Clare.

Then, as if I'd summoned her with my thoughts, I saw her, just over Daisy's bare shoulder. I blinked twice and swallowed hard, because she hadn't seen me yet. But she was really here, dressed to kill. I wanted to throw Daisy off of me and go after her, but I felt frozen in place. Then, before I could obscure myself behind Daisy's body, she saw me.

Recognition, longing, and then a hard look of resentment came my way. I expected her to run away, but she simply turned her back and talked to Megan, whom I recognized next. They were chatting with two guys from the team.

Daisy's hand was still stroking the wood in my pants when a half-baked plan began to form in my mind. Could totally backfire, but what the hell? I lifted my hips, pulled my key from my pants, and handed it to Daisy.

"Go up to my room. Two oh four. Wait for me."

I slapped her ass and she stood, walking away with enough swagger to make me take a second look. I sure as hell hoped this went the way I wanted it to.

Then I shifted my focus to Clare, whose back was still turned to me. The skin she was showing was already driving me nuts. Her shoulders and the delicate curve of her waist. I stifled a groan and went to her.

When I was close enough, I caressed the bare skin of her back. Heaven. She jolted away the second she saw me. One of the guys tried to talk to me, but I was following Clare to the front of the house before I could get a word out. I caught her in the entryway where some fresh autumn air gusted in, giving me enough room to breathe.

"Clare. Listen." I turned her by her arm, forcing her to look at me.

She lifted her chin proudly and folded her arms across her chest. "Listen? I'd listen if you ever felt like talking. What happened, Eric? Was I so easily forgotten?"

She was trying to sound tough, but her emotions showed in the tremble of her lips and the wavering tone of those few words. She was hurt, and I was fully responsible for it.

"I was trying to give you some space, Clare. It's our first few weeks here."

"You're trying to make excuses so you can fuck other girls."

She pointed back into the house. I knew she meant Daisy. She had every reason to be suspicious and pissed as hell. I'd demanded her fidelity and never promised my own.

"I haven't been with anyone since you."

"You're a liar." She spoke through gritted teeth.

I banded an arm around her waist and pressed her hard against the wall, bringing my hips flush against hers. God, she felt good. The need to have her under me was fierce. "Call me a liar again, Clare, and I'll fuck you so hard you won't be able to walk for a week."

She was a breath away, our lips nearly touching. She exhaled shakily but didn't dare repeat the accusation.

Finally, I spoke again, harnessing all my willpower not to kiss this conversation away. Because she needed to hear me out.

"You're the only one I want, believe me. I want to come home from class and see you there on my bed, ready for my dick. I want your cunt wrapped around me morning, noon, and night. You're all I fucking think about. I'll be lucky if I don't fail out from having my mind between your legs all goddamn day."

She blinked and searched me with those beautiful blue eyes. "Then why have you been ignoring me?"

"I'm not—" I sighed. "Clare, we're in college. Believe me when I say I want you all to myself, but the longer we're here, the more I realize that it's not fair of me to ask that of you. I fucked around for years at Ridgeville. You're here, finally coming into your own, on this campus with thousands of people. And you're beautiful, Clare. You're ripe for experience, and I don't want to be the one to deny you that."

She shook her head, her expression taut with emotion. "You're wrong."

"I'm right. And don't for one second think that means I don't want to be part of those experiences, but..."

"But you want your freedom too," she whispered tightly, as if she were bracing herself for something terrible.

"I'm a quarterback for a Division One football team. Doesn't matter how loyal I am to you, I'm going to have girls falling all over me. Every weekend, after every game."

She closed her eyes like what I was saying was painful. I had to open her eyes, in more ways than one.

"Don't you want more before you decide to lock things down with me, Clare? I mean, you've only been with me and Travis and..."

The guilty look in her eye told me she'd been with that surfer in Hawaii too. I could only hope he'd respected her, even as the thought of him fucking my girl sent a jealous rage through me. Except my jealousy was the problem I'd been trying to avoid for weeks by staying away from Clare. I couldn't dance around this anymore.

"Believe me, I don't want to share you with anyone. I never have. But for your sake, I think we should keep ourselves...open."

She shook her head, her gaze steady on me. "What does that mean?"

"Come with me." I grabbed her hand and took her through the party.

She offered a quick wave in Megan's direction before I led her up the stairs to my dorm room. When I opened the door, Daisy was on the bed, peeling through a magazine, her legs swinging back and forth.

She flipped over and froze when she saw Clare with me. She went to move, but I held up my hand. "Stay. Daisy, this is Clare. Clare's my girl from back home."

She bit her lip and eyed Clare cautiously. Clare stood in place like she was made of stone. I'd loosen her up, soon enough. I moved behind her, positioning her back to my front so she could feel my heat, my love. Was it love? Yeah... I couldn't really deny that anymore, but telling her now wouldn't get us over this hurdle. Mine was a twisted backward kind of love, but I'd never felt this way about anyone else. I leaned in and kissed the place where her jaw met her neck and felt her sigh in my arms.

"Three things, Daisy," I said, never glancing in the blonde's direction.

"Shoot."

"First, do you like girls?"

I flickered my gaze over to see her smirk.

"My sorority girls and I get together sometimes. We have fun."

"Good. That brings me to my second point. I want you to help me make Clare happy tonight. If you do a good job of it, I'll make you really fucking happy too."

She licked her lips while I continued my assault on Clare's neck. I could feel her muscles take turns, melting and tensing through this delicate conversation.

"What's the third thing?"

I slid my hand down the front of Clare's tight jeans, finding the damp pussy I missed so much. Sucking her earlobe and breathing in her heavenly scent, I ignored Daisy's last request for a second longer.

"I'm in charge," I finally said, leaving no doubt in my tone.

Clare weakened back into me, rolling her hips into my touch. Good. We could do this... I could show her that we could do this. Without wasting another second, I told Daisy to strip. As she did, I made short work of divesting Clare of her skin-tight party clothes. She was hot wearing them, but I preferred her naked. She had a beautiful body, and as the thought floated across my brain, an unexpected feeling of pride washed over me. I wanted to show her off. I might actually enjoy sharing her more than I expected to.

CLARE

My heart was speeding out of control. This was all happening too fast. I hadn't had a second to process Eric's words earlier. I still couldn't tell if this was an elaborate ruse to get me to accept his infidelities or if he was serious about embracing mine. He'd always been so possessive. How could he have flipped that switch so easily? Could he really accept me...experimenting? I recognized the pained expression in his eyes when he'd said the words, but then there was something else. Arousal and determination.

Once I was naked, he tossed me onto the bed next to an equally nude Daisy. Her breasts were fuller, her nipples large, rose-colored disks, while mine were smaller and lighter. Her skin was darker, though I suspected from a tanning bed and not from the summer sun. Before I could let the comparisons run rampant in my mind, Eric's touch demanded my attention. His eyes held a haze of lust and nameless emotion.

"Daisy," he said, his gaze never leaving mine, "I want you to get Clare comfortable. And wet. I want her drenched for me."

I struggled to bring air into my lungs. Then Daisy brought her hand to my cheek, turning me toward her smiling face.

"Hi," she whispered before pulling me into a kiss.

The contact was strange to start—not nearly as strong or dominant as the kisses I'd experienced from the men I'd been with. She tasted sweet, like strawberry lip gloss, and while her motions were less invasive, they were also very sensual. She pushed me back gently and spread her attentions all over my skin, bringing my nerve endings alive in the ways I'd been craving for so long. Weeks...

Eric left the foot of the bed and disappeared into his bathroom, emerging a minute later. He dropped a bottle and a few condoms onto the bed and began to undress. As each garment fell, I appreciated more of the gorgeous body beneath. Damn, I'd missed him. I almost forgot about Daisy's mouth on me until she spread my legs and brought her lips around my clit.

I sucked in a breath with a shuddery tremble. God, I was strung tight. And Daisy wasn't being gentle anymore. She was sucking and licking me with a vigor that I never would have anticipated when we'd first started. I closed my eyes and fell into the sensations, moaning and moving my hips to the pace of her intimate kisses.

"Fuck, that's hot." A raspy voice broke me out of the moment.

Eric was stroking his rock-hard cock, his eyes blazing with lust. Whatever pleasure I was feeling seemed to echo through my beautiful man. Fuck was right. I wanted him more than I ever had.

I didn't have to ask when he dropped a knee onto the bed and positioned himself beside me. He kissed my neck, biting and marking me. Combined with Daisy's stellar oral skills, I was already on edge, ready to come as soon as Eric gave me permission.

Then he lifted my leg and hooked it over his muscular thigh, turning my body away from him a fraction. A crinkle of a condom and a sound of something squirting. Then he was notched at my ass. He kissed my neck again.

"Fucking you hard here, baby. Because you're not going to last long and neither am I. Daisy, you keep sucking my sweet Clare. Keep that clit nice and swollen but don't let her come until I say."

He pushed into me then. A few careful strokes and I acclimated to his girth stretching me.

"Can I put my fingers in her pussy?" Daisy's voice was breathy with desire.

"Yes," I uttered in unison with Eric. I clenched against his cock. A new surge of my arousal coated Daisy's lips as I surrendered, finally and completely, to what Eric wanted for us. This... And now we wanted the same thing.

She pushed her fingers into me, making me more aware of all the ways I was being stimulated.

"Like a glove," she said with a giggle, shoving gently in and out.

I was sliding off the cliff fast now. "Eric. Eric, please..." I pleaded, my hips moving of their own volition.

"Soon, sweet Clare. So fucking soon." He thrust fast and hard, his breathing ragged at my ear. "Daisy, is Clare's clit swollen?"

"Oh yeah. Nice and big." She flicked her tongue over it.

"Bite it. Fuck her with your fingers. Make my girl come nice and hard."

Daisy didn't answer but did exactly what Eric wanted. I was there in a second, coming so hard I was screaming Eric's name. The sound reverberated off the walls of the small room, but I didn't care. He was the reason for my pleasure, and the world could know it.

Eric slipped out of me but Daisy continued toying with me gently, careful not to touch the most sensitive places that were still humming from my release.

Eric's voice interrupted the fog of my post-orgasmic state. "I'm going to take care of Daisy now, love."

My heart twisted at the last word. I was all sensation and nerve endings right now, but my love for Eric pulsed under all of it. I nodded, because even though he hadn't worded a question, I knew he was asking me. He couldn't do this without me, and I didn't want to ruin what we'd just shared. I trusted him.

He rose gingerly and replaced the condom on his still engorged cock with a new one. He slapped Daisy's ass, prompting her to lift it for him. She stayed stationed at my pussy, dedicated to her task, even if I was too blitzed to think about coming a second time. With one violent motion he was inside her. She cried out and fisted her hands in the comforter on either side of my thighs. Her jaw fell and our gazes met, as if we were silently bonding over the singular pleasure of enjoying Eric Hayward's beautiful cock.

The strain on Eric's expression told of his restraint. Pleasing two of us was likely a challenge in stamina for him, but he was close. By the flushed look on Daisy's face, she was too. I was still buzzing with satisfaction, but registered a little flicker of arousal in my clit watching them go at it. I was rooting for their pleasure. I wanted Eric to come hard, because I'd gotten him there and Daisy could take him the rest of the way.

I started fingering myself, and the second I did, Eric's eyes flashed open.

"Daisy," was all he said.

Then Daisy was buried in my pussy again, sucking and moaning against me, her lips and tongue pushing against me to the time of Eric's hips slamming against hers. In one explosive moment, we all came.

We collapsed on the bed, catching our breath. We were a mess, covered in the evidence of our major fuck-fest.

My head buzzed as the reality of what just happened sank in. Is this what Eric meant when he said he wanted to keep things open between us? Could I really do this?

I *had* done it. And I'd loved it. So, I guessed the answer was yes.

I was in college, and I was going to have the fucking time of my life.

CHAPTER SIX

CLARE

I hated Tuesday and Thursday afternoons. I wanted to choke my roommate, Lacey, for talking me into taking this course with her. Human Sexuality had seemed like an interesting class at registration, but it had proven to be the most agonizing hour and a half of my life. Most days, it was all I could do to stay awake long enough to take notes. Last week, Mrs. Hendrix's lecture on masturbation had been about as captivating as watching paint dry. I could only imagine how interesting today would be.

When I entered the lecture hall, I was caught off guard by the loud chaos that greeted me. Sadly, this was probably the most excitement my class had seen all semester. Dropping my backpack on the floor, I settled into my upper-level seat beside Lacey. Our professor was missing from her usual spot behind the podium. Leaning over, I tapped my roommate on the shoulder, interrupting her conversation with a group of girls.

"Hey, what's going on? Where's Mrs. Hendrix?"

Lacey spun around to face me, her dark eyes widening in disbelief. "Oh my God, you haven't heard?"

"Heard what?" Since all of my extra time was spent either tutoring or studying in the library, I was typically the very last person to know anything.

"They fired Mrs. Hendrix."

"What? Why?"

Lacey shrugged her shoulders. "I don't know. They escorted her off the campus this morning, so it must be something pretty bad."

I blinked hard, trying to process what she was saying. "Wow. I wonder who they're going to get to replace her?"

I'd barely gotten out the words when the room fell silent, every head turning toward the front of the class. Lacey's audible gasp pretty much summed up the glorious sexiness that strode confidently across the room.

The handsome, dark-haired stranger looked like he'd stepped off the cover of *GQ Magazine.* He was young, maybe in his late twenties or early thirties. His tall, athletic build reminded me a lot of Eric's, except this guy was a bit taller. A white button-up shirt and black dress pants hugged his sculpted frame as if they had been custom tailored for him. My dirty mind was already imagining how deliciously ripped he had to be beneath them.

Just when I thought this guy couldn't get any hotter, he lifted his head, revealing his pale-colored eyes, which practically glowed against his olive skin.

Who was *this guy?*

"Good afternoon, everyone. My name is Malcolm Drake. I will be taking over Mrs. Hendrix's class for the rest of the semester." His deep, seductive voice sent a wave of chills over me.

"Fucking hell, where did they find this guy? Sex-R-Us?" Lacey whispered, earning a chuckle from me.

I glanced back in his direction, still grinning from Lacey's comment. He was looking directly at me, paralyzing me in my seat. Our intense stare off seemed to go on forever, even though I'm sure it only lasted a few seconds. When he finally averted his eyes to the other side of the room, I felt a wave of relief rush over me, like a spell was broken.

I slouched in my seat, kept my head down, and pulled my notebook closer to me. As he began the lecture, my thoughts began to drift.

Before I knew it, the loud dismissal bell snapped me out of my daze. I blinked hard, my eyes slowly focusing on the screen full of notes in front of the classroom.

Shit. I'd never zoned out in class like this before. Somehow I'd latched onto the seductive tone of Mr. Drake's voice but managed not to absorb a single word he'd said. I stared down at the empty page in my notebook and cursed inwardly again.

Mr. Drake raised his voice to speak above the loud shuffling in the room. "Remember, your research papers are due this Thursday."

Rattled by my unexpected reaction to the new professor, I shoved my things into my backpack and slung it over my shoulder. I rushed out of the room and down the small set of stairs before Lacey had a chance to stop me. Once I was far enough down the hall, I ducked into a nearby bathroom, relieved to find it empty. I dropped my bag and stumbled back against the door.

If I'd thought Mrs. Hendrix's lectures were agony, enduring the rest of the semester with her replacement would be certain torture. Professor Drake was anything but dull, but he was...distracting. How in the hell was I going to make it through another eight weeks of school with him as my instructor?

◆ ◆ ◆ ◆

After a week, I couldn't deny that Human Sexuality had become my favorite class.

I bit down on the top of my pencil and sighed at the beautiful man standing in front of the classroom. His black button-up shirt hugged the toned body beneath. I couldn't imagine its perfection, but I certainly tried...

God, it should be against the law for professors to be this hot. How was I supposed to learn anything in this environment?

I wasn't the only one who shared the same sentiment. I couldn't believe some of the scandalous outfits that were now being worn to class by my classmates. Between the excessive amount of cleavage and ass they were showing, I was surprised Mr. Drake could concentrate on teaching at all. But his demeanor never changed, as if he were completely oblivious to how people lusted after him.

I would have assumed he was gay, but the heated looks I'd received from him in the hallway and in class made me think differently. I was a student and he was a teacher, and I should've been a little disturbed by those looks. But I wasn't. I found myself looking forward to our silent exchanges...a lot.

"Miss Winston."

The mention of my name snapped me from my inappropriate thoughts. In a class of over eighty-five students, I was shocked that he already knew my name. Straightening up in my seat, I locked eyes with him. I struggled to form a response.

"Yes, sir?"

A small smile crept across his gorgeous face. "Perhaps you can explain to the class what view the Ancient Greeks held on masturbation?"

A rush of heat filled my face as every head in the classroom turned in my direction. I was just opening my mouth to answer him when the dismissal bell rang.

Relieved, I shrunk back into my seat.

"It appears you are saved by the bell, Miss Winston." Mr. Drake's dark stare never wavered from mine as he continued to speak. "Be sure to read over the next two chapters. Your papers will be returned to you in class on Thursday. Good day."

The class became loud with movement as people rose to leave.

Lacey piped up beside me. "What the hell was that about?"

I shoved my binder into my bag and shrugged, trying to seem unaffected. "I don't know. I guess he wanted to embarrass me for not paying attention."

Lacey smirked. "Well, judging by how red you still are, I'd say he succeeded."

I rolled my eyes and stood. "Let's get out of here."

"Don't you want to go demonstrate your view on masturbation?"

Little did she know, her playful teasing only added another fantasy to the few I'd already been nursing for the sexy professor.

"Shut it, Lacey," I snapped.

"What? I'd gladly play naughty student any day with him."

She bit her lip as she stared toward the front of the classroom. I followed her gaze, no less immune to Professor Drake's sex appeal and the dirty fantasies he inspired.

But that's all they were... Fantasies.

◆ ◆ ◆ ◆

The large red F circled at the top of my paper seemed to leap off the page, and the crushing disappointment had nearly slapped me in the face. In all my years of school, I'd never received less than an A-on *anything*. With trembling hands, I flipped through my research paper, desperately searching for some sort of explanation. Other than the grade on the front, there wasn't a single mark or notation in the entire paper. Obviously, Mr. Drake had made some sort of mistake.

Gathering my things, I waited until everyone had left before I made my way down to the lower level. When Mr. Drake didn't acknowledge me, I stepped closer to his desk and cleared my throat to get his attention.

"Excuse me, Mr. Drake?"

I held my breath, watching as he slowly raised his head. The instant his icy blue eyes locked with mine, I froze. From this close up, he was even more breathtaking, which made keeping myself together very difficult.

"Can I help you with something, Miss Winston?"

Petrified by his intimidating demeanor, I struggled to speak. "Y-Yes, sir. I think there may be some sort of mistake with my grade." My hands were shaking when I laid my paper on the desk in front of him.

He raised his brow. "I see."

He briefly lifted the paper, glanced at the front page, and tossed it back on his desk. I had to bite the inside of my lip to control my irritation.

"There's no mistake, Miss Winston. The grade is correct," he replied dryly, returning his attention to his writing.

No, no, no!

My stomach plummeted. I'd spent countless hours in the library working on it, following every single guideline that was listed in the syllabus. How could I possibly have gotten a failing grade on it?

"But, sir, there isn't anything marked to explain the grade you gave me."

He threw his pen down onto the desk. "The execution of your paper was flawless, Miss Winston, but that isn't the point."

Unless the "F" on my paper meant flawless, I was completely lost on what he was saying.

"I don't understand," I replied, this time more urgent with my tone.

"No, you're right, Miss Winston. You don't understand. *That's* the problem."

"Excuse me?" I was both shocked and angered by his accusation. "I spent a lot of time researching the topic, Mr. Drake. Believe me, I understood the assignment completely."

He raised his hand to stop me. "You see, that's where you're wrong, Miss Winston. You can read every book and article ever written on human sexuality, but that doesn't make you an expert on it. The sources you cited were safe and far too predictable. I'm interested in *your* experiences, *your* views." He nodded toward the paper lying in front of him. "Not an ounce of your work tells me you have a handle on this topic beyond regurgitating the facts that others have written about."

Why was he being so unreasonable?

"Can I at least have another opportunity on this assignment?"

"I'm afraid not."

"Please, sir. Even if I ace the final exam, this failing paper means my grade for the class won't be higher than a D." The desperation in my voice was undeniable.

Mr. Drake eyed me hard, his jaw tensing. "And? I fail to see how that is my problem."

Heavy tears pooled in my eyes. "I'll lose my scholarship, Mr. Drake. I won't be able to afford the tuition to come back to school in the spring." I tasted the salty tears as they poured down my face. "Please, I'm begging you."

Something dark glimmered in his icy blue eyes. I wasn't sure I liked it.

"Begging is beneath you, Clare," he said, his tone dangerously low.

I exhaled sharply, realizing that he'd just called me by my first name. The power in his stare was making my body react in ways it shouldn't. He was my teacher. I was his student. This was crossing every line of what was appropriate.

"Desperation is a dangerous emotion. It pushes people to do things they wouldn't normally do in order to get what they want." He tilted his head, studying me. "Are you willing to be pushed, Clare?"

Pushed? Pushed to do what?

"I'm a hard worker. If you give me a chance, I'll prove that to you." Keeping my chin up, I stood before him, knowing that the fate of my scholarship rested solely in his hands. I was utterly at his mercy, if he had any.

A few agonizing seconds passed, the air between us thick with unexplainable tension.

"Okay, Clare. If I agree to grant you the extra credit in this class, it's with the understanding that you'll never question me, or my methods. If, at any time, you hesitate to do as you're told, the deal is off. Is that clear?"

Hope filled me, and I blinked away the sting of my earlier tears. "Yes, sir."

"Very good. Meet me here at seven o'clock tomorrow night—not a second later. I'm bending the rules, because I see great potential in you. Don't make me regret it."

"I won't, sir. I promise. Thank you," I rushed.

A wicked smirk graced his handsome face as he handed me back my paper. "Don't thank me yet, Miss Winston. You don't know what I have in store for you."

I bit my lip with an uncertain nod. I wasn't sure what I had just agreed to, but I had the unsettling feeling that I may have just sold my soul to the devil.

ERIC

"But this was our weekend."

I groaned into the phone, unable to mask my disappointment. Two weeks had gone by since I'd tasted Clare, and I was dying to make up for lost time. This was a bye week for our team, which was perfect since my roommate had plans to be out of town for the entire weekend. My plan had been to spend as much time inside Clare Winston as possible.

"I know, Eric. I'm really sorry to have to cancel, but I've got a ton of homework to do."

Something was definitely off in her voice. Was she blowing me off for another guy? It was Friday, for fuck's sake. Who in their right mind did homework on a Friday night?

Frustrated, I ran my hands through my hair. "Just be honest with me, Clare. Are you seeing someone else?" I held my breath, terrified of what her answer would be.

"What? No, of course not!"

Her answer sent a wave of relief over me.

"Then, tell me what's going on. Something's wrong."

She blew out a long breath into the phone. "Nothing's wrong, Eric. I'm just really overwhelmed. My tutoring job at the library is taking up so much of my time that I've fallen behind on some of my assignments. That's all."

"I need to see you, Clare. Just thirty minutes, please." Hell, if she'd just give me five goddamn minutes, I'd show her how quickly I could make her come. I knew her pussy like the back of my hand. It would only take five seconds of my tongue pressing her clit, and I'd have her screaming out my name.

"Eric," she whispered into the phone.

I cursed inwardly. Deep down, I knew she wasn't going to meet me for a quickie. There was only one other option... Phone sex.

CLARE

Damn it. Of all nights, why did I pick tonight to let Eric talk me into having phone sex?

I sprinted down the hall, crossing the threshold of the classroom just as the time on my phone changed to seven p.m. Panting, I smoothed down my hair, hoping that the blush from my earlier orgasm had finally disappeared from my face.

"Cutting it close, aren't we?"

Professor Drake's deep voice boomed from the darkened level above me, sending a shockwave through me. Squinting, I looked up into the balcony, barely catching the silhouette of his body. Before I could speak, he issued his first demand.

"Have a seat in front of my desk, Miss Winston."

I situated myself on the wooden chair, tugging my skirt down. I shifted nervously in my seat as he approached. He strode confidently around me and sat on the edge of the desk, facing me.

"Are you ready to begin?" He smirked, loosening his tie.

"Yes, sir." I reached for my textbook, but he stopped me, lifting a hand and shaking his head.

"You won't be needing that." He hardened his stare before continuing. "Let's just say that what I'm about to teach you doesn't exactly go along with the university's approved curriculum."

I swallowed hard, trying to calm my racing heart. I didn't know what he had in mind for this lesson, but so far, I was scared shitless. He was my professor. Surely he wouldn't do anything to risk losing his job. Then again, we were both risking something by being here.

"For you to earn this extra credit, I have to know you have a true understanding of the topics, Clare. Your paper was safe, and frankly, boring. I know you're capable of better. If you want to prove that, you have to be willing to push past your insecurities. Do you think you can do that?"

When I nodded, he stood and dimmed the lights above me, until we were in complete darkness. My heart wouldn't slow as I waited for what he'd do next. Seconds later, the overhead projector switched on, illuminating the white screen that hung from the ceiling.

"I want you to pay close attention to every single detail of the video you're about to watch. When it's done, I will test you on it."

Even without the benefit of seeing him, I found the sound of his voice erotic. Confident, low, and hypnotic.

Suddenly, the screen above me came to life. I gasped at the figure of a naked woman projected onto the screen, spread eagle, leaving nothing to the imagination. Within a few seconds, I realized I was watching porn. The woman licked her fingers and worked the moisture over her clit, moving feverishly in circular motions. My face heated as my own body began reacting to what I saw. The woman's moans grew louder and louder, until she threw her head back and screamed, her body shaking from her orgasm. The muscles in my neck strained as I resisted the urge to look away.

The camera zoomed in on her sex just as she sank her fingers into her pussy and worked them in a frenzied pace. As I turned my head away, the professor's strong hands cupped my face from behind and turned me back.

"Watch her, Clare." His breath was warm against my ear.

I squirmed in my seat, squeezing my thighs together.

"Pay attention to how your body reacts. It's natural. Don't fight it." He released his hold on my face and gripped the sides of my arms, gently pinning me back against the chair. "Look at her face, Clare. Feel her pleasure as if it were your own."

I exhaled sharply, noting how hard my nipples had suddenly become inside my bra. The pressure between my legs was now unbearable. Moaning, I shifted in the chair, trying to alleviate the discomfort.

"Tell me, Clare. When you're alone in your dorm at night, do you touch yourself?"

"Yes." I closed my eyes, feeling heat rush to my cheeks with the confession.

The woman on the screen was still moaning and breathing heavily, adding to the forbidden arousal pooling between my thighs.

The professor released his hold on me, and I heard his footsteps circle in front of me. When he lifted my chin, I opened my eyes. His gaze was dark with desire.

"Your shyness will be your downfall, Clare. How will you learn if you don't push yourself?" His gaze flickered down my body. "Spread your legs."

The voice in my head told me to run while I still had the chance, before I crossed every line that had the potential to destroy me. But I no longer had the choice to run, and I wasn't sure I would, even if I could. If anyone walked in and saw this, I would be expelled from school. The thought of getting caught was thrilling, though, and that momentarily outweighed my fear.

With his smoldering stare still fixed on me, I scooted to the edge of the chair and inched my skirt up, spreading my legs without taking my eyes off him.

"Put your feet on the edge of my desk and lean back."

I did as he asked, and when his mouth fell open slightly, I knew he could see everything. I had rushed to his classroom after Eric's dirty words had put me over the edge. And now I wasn't wearing anything beneath my skirt.

"Are you ready for your test?" he rasped, licking his lips.

"Yes, sir," I whispered.

The woman on the screen was getting louder. She was close, and hell if I didn't feel like I was a touch away from coming myself.

As if he could sense my inner turmoil, the professor tensed his jaw and straightened. "It's time to erase all of your inhibitions."

He held up a small remote and aimed it toward the projector to pause the video. I stared up at the still image of the woman, her face frozen in mid-climax.

He pointed to the screen. "Do you see that girl? I want you to become her. Touch yourself. Show me how you make yourself come."

Closing my eyes, I eased my hand downward, until my fingertips brushed my bare pussy. I inched them downward, coating them with my arousal.

"Taste yourself, Clare. Learn how sweet your cunt is."

Trembling, I knew I was about to venture into unfamiliar territory, but the idea excited me more than it scared me. Everything about Professor Drake seemed to fall into that category suddenly. Following his command, I brought my fingers up to my mouth and slipped them between my lips. My tongue swirled over the pads of my fingertips.

"How do you taste? Describe it to me."

I thought for a moment, my mind racing to find the exact words. "Salty. Sweet. Delicious."

He nodded slightly. "Good girl. Now close your eyes for me."

As I did, I could feel my heart pounding in my chest. Whatever test this was, I was enjoying every minute of it. Heaven help me, I hoped I would pass.

"Imagine your lover between your thighs, staring at you. Tasting you, just as you did. Devouring every last drop of your arousal, until you're writhing with need."

I moaned quietly, the image of Eric between my legs triggering a heavy ache in my core. I dropped my hand down and worked my fingertips around my wet sex.

"Good. Now, imagine his long fingers slowly sinking inside of you... Fucking you hard. That's what you want, right?"

"Yes," I whimpered, letting the fantasy play out behind my eyelids. I pushed my fingers deep into my pussy with a groan, working them in and out in a fevered rush.

"Good. Very good." His voice was like velvet, smooth and textured at once. "I'm so hard right now, Clare. Open your legs wider. Let me see you fuck that beautiful wet cunt."

I increased my pace, my lips trembling. "Oh, God. I'm going to come."

"That's it. Listen to your body. Don't fight it."

I was close...so close. Then I heard a loud growl and opened my eyes.

My beautiful professor stood a few feet away, his dress slacks unzipped and his cock in his hand. The sight of him pumping and stroking himself toward climax sent me over. Leaning back in the chair, I gave in to the overwhelming sensation. I came hard, gasping and crying out as the woman in the video had, too wrapped up in the moment to hold back.

After a few sobering breaths, I lowered my gaze back to Professor Drake. He leaned back against his desk, working his cock faster and faster. Judging from the look on his face, I knew he was about to come. I licked my lips as a feeling of pride washed over me.

I couldn't wait to watch, to know I'd done this to him.

"Get on your knees, Clare."

His heavy-lidded gaze held a question with the demand. I only considered it a moment before I dropped to my knees.

He came toward me, his muscles tight with strain, the skin taut over his cock as he stroked it. "I'm going to come all over your pretty little face."

His free hand wrapped around my long ponytail, yanking my head back in one forceful movement. His words and roughness caused me to moan, and I had the inexplicable urge to wrap my lips around his cock and finish him off until he roared.

"Fuck!" He threw his head back as warm spurts of semen landed across my mouth, coating my lips.

I sucked in my bottom lip with a smile, savoring the salty flavor as it hit my tongue. He tasted different than Eric, but still every bit as delicious.

After a few moments, he collapsed back against his desk, struggling to catch his breath. I sighed with satisfaction. There was no doubt about it.

Today's grade would be an A.

ERIC

Bored out of my mind, I braced my head up with my hand and stared at the large flat-screen television on the wall. I could think of a million fucking things I would rather be doing on a Saturday night than sitting with a bunch of guys watching *Fast and Furious 7*, again! I was half asleep when I heard one of my fraternity brothers let out a loud curse.

"Goddamn."

I turned my head, my mouth dropping at the goddess who walked through the door. Clare sauntered toward me, seducing me with every move of her hips and the dangerously short black dress that clung to them. Her long legs looked like they went on for miles. When my eyes landed on the silver stilettos on her feet, I groaned. I fucking wanted those around my neck tonight.

I pushed off the couch to my feet. "Clare? What are you doing here?"

She eyed the other guys in the room. "Get out," she ordered with a flick of her hand and an authority I'd never heard from her before.

Without another word, the room cleared, leaving the two of us alone.

Whoever this girl was, I fucking loved her.

"Clare? What are you—"

Before I could finish my question, she placed both of her hands on my chest and shoved me backward onto the couch. I barely hit the cushions before she was climbing over me, straddling me. Her newfound confidence had me speechless. Where was my shy Clare?

Grinning at her little game, I placed my hands on her hips and then inched them down to cup her ass. She grabbed my wrists, halting my journey. The sides of her mouth slowly lifted, turning into a sly smirk as she shook her head.

"No touching, Mr. Hayward. Tonight, I'm in charge."

In one forceful move, the beautiful vixen shoved my hands above my head, surprising me with her strength. She leaned into me, stopping when her plump lips brushed against mine. Unable to control myself, I lifted my head to kiss her, but she shifted her weight, tightening her grip around my wrists.

"Don't. Move. Understand?"

My cock swelled. I had no idea where the whole dominatrix act came from, but I was loving it. Anytime she wanted to have a taste of control, I'd gladly give her the reins.

"Yes, ma'am."

Clare slowly traced her tongue across the seam of my lips. "Good boy," she whispered, releasing me from her grasp. My eyes were instantly drawn to her exposed cleavage, where the outline of her erect nipples strained against the fabric of her dress. Shifting my jaw, I could practically feel the hard pink bud between my teeth.

"Baby, let's take this to my room. Anyone can walk in on us here."

"I don't care. Let them watch."

Before I could talk her out of it, Clare gripped the top of her dress and yanked the material down until her luscious tits bounced free in front of me. Staring confidently into my eyes, my beautiful seductress took each swollen nipple between her fingers, twisting and pulling until she was whimpering with pleasure.

Her eyes glimmered when I growled. "Like what you see?"

"Fuck, yes." My mouth watered with the thought of having her breasts against my lips, her rosy lips on my tongue. I parted my lips, inviting her closer, but she didn't bite.

I lifted my hips, hoping to give her a taste of her own medicine. I rotated my hips until my engorged cock pressed against her core and held her in place. All that separated us were my thin exercise shorts.

Raising her brows, she pressed her hands against my chest and shoved me back down. "Uh-huh, Mr. Hayward." She lifted her body off me, stood, and grabbed my jaw. "Remember, *I'm* the one calling the shots."

Mischief danced in Clare's eyes as she released my face. Twisting her hips back and forth, she inched up her skirt until I was staring at her beautiful bare pussy.

Easing herself down onto the edge of the ottoman behind her, she pushed her hands between her thighs, spreading herself open for me.

Without diverting her smoldering gaze, she massaged her fingers against her glistening pink folds in slow circular motions.

Fuck. I bit the inside of my lip, dying for permission to join in.

"If you want this, Eric, you're going to have to work for it." She lifted her fingers to her mouth and sucked the arousal from each one.

I swallowed hard, trying to keep myself composed. I would have gladly crawled through fire just to have a little taste.

"Show me how hard you are for me."

I reached for the waistband of my shorts. The instant I pulled them past my hips, my dick sprang free from its confinement. I gripped the base of my shaft and leaned back against the cushion, savoring the erotic show in front of me. Clare sank her fingers into her pussy. *Jesus Christ.* The heaviness in my balls was killing me. I honestly didn't know how much longer I was going to be able to hold back at this rate.

She crooked a finger, urging me to come to her. That was all the permission I needed. I lunged forward and placed my hands on the ottoman to brace me as I stared down into her heated eyes.

"I'm so wet for you, Eric. I want you to fuck me."

Desperate to be inside her, I kissed her lips, savoring the sweet taste of her pussy that still lingered on them. "Let me grab a condom, baby." I panted, pushing up off the cushion.

She stopped me by grabbing my arm. "No, Eric."

I frowned.

"I want to feel you bare, but I have to know I can trust you with my body."

Swallowing hard, I allowed myself to process what she was saying. I already knew that Clare was on the pill, but this was something we hadn't discussed before. She had already given her innocence to me. Now, she was willing to give me more.

This was a dangerous line we were about to cross—a line that would only deepen what I was feeling for her. As I stared into her eyes, I knew that being with her was worth every risk I would take with my heart.

"I just got tested a couple of weeks ago at my football physical. I'm clean. I swear." That was the truth. When it came to sex, I had always been careful. No matter how heated the moment had gotten with a girl, I'd never once gone without wrapping it up. It was a cardinal rule of mine. But one I would gladly break for her.

Clare flashed me a coy smile and then rolled onto her stomach. I stroked my length, watching as she positioned herself on all fours and lifted her ass high in the air. I hissed, the temptation to fuck her delicate pink hole nearly overwhelming me.

I moved to her, unable to resist the urge to sink my thumb past the tight ring of muscle. I'd only been there once before, but I couldn't stop thinking about having her there again. She clenched around the small invasion, and my eyes nearly rolled back in my head.

"Fuck me in the ass, Eric. Show me how rough you can be."

I hesitated only a second. She wasn't being shy tonight. Clare knew exactly what she wanted, and I was going to give it to her.

I gathered spit in my mouth and then parted my lips enough to allow a long stream of saliva to escape. My aim was perfect, and a dollop landed on the opening of her ass. Gripping the base of my shaft, I dipped the tip of my cock into the pool of my spit and then worked the moisture up my length. I aligned my dick to her opening, holding my breath as I carefully sank inside.

The searing heat of her tight cavity felt like fucking heaven. There was something so powerful about being inside her body, raw and unprotected. I caught one of her wrists and held it to her back as I gave one final shove, loudly cursing once I was fully seated.

The heavy ache in my balls was torture. I dropped her hand, stilling for a moment to try to gain composure. But the way Clare was writhing made it impossible for me to ignore her urgency. I pulled out of her and then pushed forward, gritting my teeth. Her tight sphincter muscles clamped around me as I struggled to regain entrance to her body. I closed my eyes and rocked her hips back and forth against me. Each powerful thrust was so deliciously euphoric, I became more untamed with each brutal impact.

"Harder!" Clare cried out, syncing her rugged movements with mine. "Fuck." *Thrust.* "Me." *Thrust.* "Harder."

Like a savage, I grabbed the back of her long hair, yanking her toward me. The rhythmic sound of our bodies slapping against each other filled the room. Between that and her screams, there was no doubt in my mind the entire frat house could hear us fucking like animals. Hell, they were probably standing on the fucking stairway jerking off to us. I didn't give a shit. All I cared about was making sure she knew who owned this ass and ruining her from wanting anyone else. She was all fucking mine.

"Oh, God! Don't stop. I'm coming!"

I tightened my grip and kept my pace. Gritting my teeth, I tried to hold my own orgasm back, but the sensation was too overpowering.

"So. Tight. So. Fucking. Good. I'm going to come, Clare."

"Come in my ass, Eric. Fill me up."

I dropped my hands back down to her hips, digging my fingernails into her flesh as I exploded, unleashing my hot release inside her. She sank into the cushion, giving me deeper access. I pressed as hard as I could, holding her in place as I continued filling her.

Panting, I staggered backward and collapsed onto the couch. Clare's perfect round ass remained high in the air, tempting me for another round. My breath hitched at the sight before me—my release slowly made a slick wet trail from her opening, through the folds of her pussy, down her thigh onto the ottoman.

A sudden rush of pride filled my chest. I'd just marked her body, and seeing that proof was the sexiest fucking thing I'd ever seen in my life.

I glanced down at my cock, now rock hard again, and marveled at my quick recovery. Clare didn't know it just yet, but I wasn't anywhere near done with her. I wanted her upstairs, naked and tied to my bed, those strappy silver heels wrapped around my neck as I rammed into her. Since my roommate wasn't due back until late Sunday night, Clare Winston was all fucking mine for the next twenty-four hours. With my stamina, the girl would be lucky if she could walk to class on Monday.

Growling, I lunged forward, grabbed her by the waist, and tossed her over my shoulder. Her bare ass was mere inches from my face and much too enticing not to touch. I delivered a hard slap against her bottom and she yelped.

"W-What are you doing?"

"I'm taking you to my room. It's my turn to be in charge, Miss Winston."

CHAPTER SEVEN

CLARE

Not yet fully awake, I nestled against the warm body curled behind me. I felt two strong arms tighten around my midsection, and I smirked at the feel of Eric's morning arousal pressed against my ass.

Any time in Eric's presence was a gift, but waking up in his arms was quickly becoming one of my favorite things in the world. We were well into the semester by now, and while our schedules sometimes kept us apart for days at a time, we always found our way back into each other's arms, and beds.

With a quiet moan, I turned to face him.

His eyes were sleepy but glittered when his lips curved into a lazy grin. "Good morning, beautiful."

"Last night was amazing," I whispered, warming in his embrace as I recalled our all-night romp.

His silky brown hair was perfectly mussed. I ran my fingers through it gently.

He leaned down, kissing me tenderly. "*You're* amazing. I don't know how I'm supposed to leave you today."

Thanksgiving break was upon us. Most of the students on

campus, including my roommate, had gone home for the holiday. In a matter of hours, Eric would be on his way to Ridgeville, and I'd be back to missing him all over again. Missing him and worrying...

"Do you think you'll see Mandy?"

He traced my wrinkled brow, his expression never changing. "You never have to worry about her, okay?"

"You were with her a long time. I know things are...open... between us. But the idea of you being with her kills me. I can't lie."

"As long as I'm with you, you'll never have to worry about that. She's dead to me after what she did."

"She's really beautiful."

He tucked a strand of my curly hair behind my ear and stared deeply into my eyes. "So are you, Clare. And you have my heart. She never did."

I chewed at my lip and avoided his penetrating gaze. I had a hard time believing him when he said things like that. He was Eric Hayward. Homecoming king. Star quarterback. Fuck of the century. Staking claim to any part of him seemed impossible, except when we were together like this. Eye to eye, bodies entwined, memories of our wild fucking clinging to my skin like sex on sheets.

He shook his head like he could read the doubt written on my features. "I fucked you all damn night. I'm obsessed with you, woman. What more do I have to do?"

I sighed. "Nothing. Sorry, I'm being sensitive. I guess I already miss you."

"Why don't you come home with me? You shouldn't have to stay on campus all by yourself."

"I won't be alone. A few of my friends are staying in the dorms for the weekend."

"Paul?"

I lifted an eyebrow at the mention of my study partner. "Yes, Paul is staying. He lives across the country so it's easier for him to just stay here until winter break."

Eric's jaw muscles tensed, but he didn't say anything more. Paul was harmless. He'd never once made a move on me. He never partied on campus, and I doubted he'd ever dated a girl. Threat level was zero.

"I appreciate the invitation. I really do, because it's more than my dad gave me. But I don't want to be a burden. I'm sure your family is really excited to see you. Me, not so much."

"One day I want them to meet you. They'll love you." He caressed down the bridge of my nose, an affectionate gesture that twisted my heart.

These little moments with Eric were like wisps off a dandelion, precious and gone too quickly. But I'd always cherish them, no matter what happened between us.

"I hope so. Maybe another time," I said softly.

I didn't want to say it out loud, but until we were a committed couple, I didn't really want to pretend like we were. Eric and I had agreed to keep things open and enjoy whatever experiences college presented to us. And while I was definitely enjoying myself, my heart belonged to Eric Hayward and him alone. He'd always have it.

"Don't worry about me. I'll be fine," I reassured him.

His expression was serious then. "I want you to have fun, Clare. Just don't fall in love with anyone while I'm gone, okay?"

I shot him a smile that I hoped relieved him of all those worries.

"In four days? Not possible."

"Let me just make sure you don't," he said, whispering his breath down my torso until he was positioned between my thighs. "A few extra precautions to make sure this pussy stays addicted to my mouth. My cock. My fingers." He licked me and pressed two fingers deep into my heat.

"Eric!"

His answering groan vibrated through me. "Only me."

I closed my eyes and arched against his mouth. "Only you."

♦ ♦ ♦ ♦

I splurged on Thanksgiving dinner at the only Chinese restaurant in our quiet campus town with the few friends who'd stuck around—Paul, Kitty, and her boyfriend, Todd. Kitty and Todd spent most of the meal the way they spent most of our study dates—tangled up in each other like two sex-crazed primates.

If I'd never known love, I might have hated them, but I was happy to see my friends enjoying each other. Even if they made me a little lonely for Eric.

Our waiter packed up the leftovers, and I watched the sky grow dark outside.

"We're taking off, I guess," Kitty finally said, her hand tightly threaded through Todd's.

"Okay. Have a great night. Happy Thanksgiving." I glanced at Paul, who was studying the zodiac menu placemat in front of him like it was required reading. "Want to hang out for another round?"

Paul lifted his eyebrows, a slight movement that shifted both his black-rimmed glasses and his long dark bangs against his forehead.

"Uh, sure. I guess we don't have to worry about class tomorrow or anything."

I smirked. Always so cautious. If I'd asked him to come back and work ahead on our biology labs for next week, he would not have hesitated. Poor Paul needed to live a little.

I signaled the waiter, who swiftly brought us refills.

"According to this menu, I'm a goat," he said after a moment.

I giggled and leaned over his shoulder to see, though it read the same as mine. "Calm, gentle, creative, frank, and honest. Those sound like wonderful qualities, Paul. Though I wouldn't necessarily associate them with a goat."

He pursed his lips and nodded.

"Let's see. What am I?" I scanned the menu for my birth year. "A tiger. Open, brave, confident, adventurous." I made a little sound, running those adjectives around in my head a few more times. I would have never described myself that way before meeting Eric, but perhaps innately, this was who I was meant to be. Someone who wasn't afraid of herself, of rejection, of anything that veered off the path of the norm.

"You sound surprised." Paul's expression seemed a little more relaxed than I'd seen it before.

I cocked my head. "I'm not as afraid of the world as I used to be. But that's a bit of a new development."

He looked down and picked at the corner of the bottle's label.

"How about you? Do you feel like college has changed you at all?"

He shrugged, never meeting my gaze.

"Have you met anyone you're interested in on campus? In class or whatever?"

He was so still, he seemed to stop breathing. He licked his lips, which I noticed in that moment were full and dark. He brushed his hair back nervously, but when he looked up, the heat in his eyes could have knocked me on my ass.

Oh fuck.

I tried to pretend like I hadn't noticed. I cleared my throat.

"We should probably head back," I said when I caught my breath.

"Yeah," he said, tossing a stack of bills on the table and rising before I could reach for my wallet. He was already at the door, and I almost had to run to keep up with him.

We continued that way, him rushing and me struggling to keep up, all the way to campus. He only slowed down when we got to the entrance of my dorm.

"I'll see you later, I guess," he said, looking in the other direction.

"Paul." I caught the lapel on his tweed blazer and yanked, hoping to get him to look at me. "Are you mad at me?"

His jaw tightened and he stared down at his feet. "Am I mad at you? Not exactly."

"What is it? Talk to me." I slid my hand up his coat, feeling his muscular chest through it. It never occurred to me that under his conservative clothes and stellar work ethic that he was ripped...and frustrated.

He caught my wrist as I molded my palm over his pectoral. Squaring his body with mine, he pushed me against the brick of the building. "Clare Winston. I'm not mad. I'm crazy... You are driving me crazy."

Before I could say anything, his lips were pressed to mine. Hungry, seeking. In an instant, the benevolent friend I'd known had transformed into six feet of muscled desire. When his tongue probed, all reason fled and I opened for him, accepting his warm, intoxicating taste. I moaned when he positioned his thigh between my mine, putting the perfect amount of pressure against my sex.

"Paul," I gasped.

But he only pressed harder, molding our bodies together more tightly. On the empty campus, no one was there to witness our heated embrace. He kissed me hard, like I was water and he was drinking from me to survive. Had he been starved of this kind of moment his whole life? Had something about our time together unlocked this passion?

Minutes went by and my sense of propriety temporarily won out. "We need to go inside," I said, breathless from his intense kissing.

He nodded and followed me inside. I paused when I entered the small room.

A knot of guilt lodged in my stomach, in large part because of Eric's jealousy. But hadn't he been the one to tell me to have my fun, to embrace all the experiences? Would he see this as a betrayal?

Before I could dwell on it, Paul's hands were on me, turning me to him.

I looked into his eyes. Reaching up, I took off his glasses, and for the first time since I'd met him, I could truly appreciate his face. His features were chiseled, but his eyes were by far his most striking feature. An intense green with flecks of amber around the center. Ditch the nerd wardrobe and put him in a football uniform, and Paul would have girls lined up around the building.

"You're beautiful," I whispered.

He cupped my cheek. "I have to tell you something."

"What is it?"

He licked his lips and took a few short breaths. Grazing his hands down my sides, he gripped and stroked, as if he was experimenting with what I liked, what he wanted. Then I knew. He was a virgin.

"Paul... Have you ever...?"

"No, but I don't want to scare you away. I've had chances before. I just didn't want to waste the moment with someone who wasn't good enough."

I shook my head. "Why me?"

"Because you're a tiger." He smirked and leaned in for a kiss, this one softer and slower.

Seconds slipped by as we devoured each other's mouths and took our time stripping our clothes to the floor. He was down to his boxers and I was in my panties, moaning as his palms curved over my breasts.

With my eyes closed, I had a flash of Eric's face. He wasn't angry, but he was there, his presence pulsing in my heart. I sucked in a breath and stilled Paul's roaming hands. This could possibly be a terrible time to hit the brakes, but I owed it to Paul to be honest with him. As a friend, he deserved that.

He frowned. "Is everything okay?"

"You're perfect. I want this, Paul. But I have to tell you something before we go any farther."

"Tell me, because I'm about to lose my mind if I can't be inside you soon."

My heart skipped a beat when I thought about being the first one he'd ever be inside.

"Paul, I'm in love with someone else."

He froze. "I don't want to make you do something you don't want to do. I don't want to be that guy."

"You aren't, I promise. Me and Eric... Our relationship is different. We aren't exclusive. He's okay with this. But I don't want to hurt you because I can't take things to the next level after tonight."

He swallowed, the bulge in his throat bobbing with the effort. "I understand."

"You're amazing, Paul. I care about you so much. I don't want things to change if we do this."

"They won't."

"Are you sure?" I wasn't sure if I could believe him in the heat of the moment, with his hard cock pressed against my belly.

"Calm, gentle, creative, frank, and honest," he said quietly.

I smiled slowly. "A goat."

He rolled his eyes. "Whatever. I want to fuck you, Clare. And when we're done, you're still going to be one of my best friends. I'll just know what it's like to lose myself in you. I can't promise I won't ever want it again. But if we can't have it again, we can't. I'm not giving up this moment. I've waited too fucking long for it."

I'd rarely heard Paul curse. He was so precise, so deliberate and in control. I had the strong sense he was teetering on the edge of control right now, but I had no choice but to believe him. I'd barely nodded before he pushed us down onto my small twin bed. I expected him to strip us the rest of the way, but he only nestled his muscular body above me, settling his hips between my thighs. So far, there was nothing virginal about the way he touched me. My skin was on fire and my pussy was pulsing and drenched, anxious to be filled.

He pumped his hips, grinding his erection against my clit several times until I thought I might come that way. Then it occurred to me that I definitely didn't want him coming that way either. I had no idea what his stamina was, and I wanted this to be amazing for both of us. I pushed him away just enough to grab a condom from my side table.

I pushed his boxers down and took his thick cock in my hands. I stroked it slowly, taking a moment to appreciate his girth and length. God, if half the girls in our Psych class knew what Paul was working with...

I rolled on the condom and the second I was finished, he yanked my panties down and came back between my legs like he was ready to fuck me into next week. I pressed my hands to his abs, relishing how they tightened under my palms. Gazing into his eyes, I shifted my hips just enough to bring the tip of his cock into me.

"Go slow, Paul. Then you can fuck me hard and fast. But right now, I want to feel every inch of you. I want to watch you lose yourself in me for the first time."

He closed his eyes, his jaw agape, like the words that had rolled off my tongue might do him in alone. "Heaven help me, Clare. You're going to be a hard act to follow."

I licked my lips and bit the bottom one. We hadn't even gotten started.

Then he began pushing in, short breathless thrusts that joined us together a little more each time. His gaze was riveted where his cock was stretching me. A series of absent "fucks" left his lips as he buried himself deeper inside my wet pussy. I was so intent on his experience that I nearly forgot my own until he shoved home with his last thrust.

My eyes went wide, and I grabbed his toned arms to brace myself against the abrupt invasion.

He stilled. "Shit. Are you okay?"

"I'm fine. Do that again."

After a tense second he thrust again, this time with more care.

"Harder," I begged.

His jaw clamped tight, and he grabbed my hips before lunging hard.

I groaned and my eyes rolled back. Paul was big, and long, and he felt fucking amazing. "Yeah," I moaned, swiveling my hips against his. "Just like that."

I heard him exhale, and then his body was hot against mine and his cock was impaling me with hard steady thrusts. They were like his passionate kisses. His hot stare. Everything about Paul was intense.

So intense that I was coming violently in a matter of seconds. It was my turn to curse into the air, my nails digging into his hips as he drove into me with abandon. Tension and determination went to war on his features. He wanted to make this last. God love him for that.

After my first orgasm faded out, I pushed him onto his back and straddled him. While I rode him, dropping down so he filled me completely and hit that magic spot inside me over and over again, he used his new position to touch me everywhere. He pinched my nipples. Caressed my skin. Toyed with my clit until I was ready to come again.

I moaned his name as he brought me down on his cock over and over.

"Clare, fuck, I'm coming."

"Come," I whimpered. "Come for me, Paul. God, it feels so good."

His eyes closed, and he punched his hips up fiercely.

"Fuck me, Paul. I want to come hard with you." I bit my lip, knowing that my dirty words would do him in the way his enormous cock was doing me in. I cried out as the orgasm ripped through me.

He sat up so he could hold me tight, chest to chest, and thrust one last time with a grunt and his lips against my neck.

"Fucking amazing," he groaned.

The tension left his muscles and we melted into the sheets together, sated, and hopefully, still very good friends.

Midnight passed, but sleep evaded me. As Paul slumbered beside me, my phone rang with a text from Eric. I picked it up and read his message.

Miss you.

My heart twisted.

Miss you more.

Then...

Are you having fun?

I hesitated, not knowing if this was the best time to answer him. But if I didn't, he'd worry more.

Yes

A moment went by that felt like eternity. My heart raced, and I worried that maybe I'd made the wrong decision with Paul.

Are you falling in love?

I sighed and tapped out my reply quickly.

Only with you. Been that way every day for as long as I can remember.

Then...

Good. See you in a few days, beautiful Clare.

I closed my eyes and put the phone down. I turned against Paul's warm body and let sleep finally take me.

CHAPTER EIGHT

ERIC

"Give me back my phone, you little shit!"

I chased my little brother down the stairs that led into our kitchen. The nosy fucker had swiped it off my nightstand while I was in the shower. When I walked back into my room, he was sitting on the foot of my bed reading through all my text messages. God only knows what he'd seen before I caught him. He must have been looking over my shoulder earlier when I entered my passcode.

"Hayden, give your brother back his phone this instant," my mother scolded.

Even though he gave me back my phone, the devious look in his eyes told me he wasn't letting this go. At twelve years old, he was already a goddamn monster.

"Eric's got a girlfriend!" he sang throughout the kitchen.

In unison, both my parents' heads shot up with wide-eyed stares.

"When did this happen? Did you meet someone at school? What's her name?" My mom's questions were coming at me like the rapid fire of a machine gun.

"Jesus, Mom!"

"Her name's Clare Winston," Hayden announced from across the room.

Narrowing my eyes, I shot him a death glare. The little fucker better not close his eyes while I was home on break. He was definitely losing both his eyebrows when I got a hold of him.

"Winston? That name sounds familiar. Where's she from?" My dad laid his newspaper down and adjusted his glasses.

Great. Now he was getting in on the interrogation.

I cleared my throat and decided to dive in. "She's from Ridgeville. We went to high school together."

"Eric Alexander Hayward! Just when exactly were you planning on telling us about her?"

I rolled my eyes. "Mom, Clare and I aren't officially a couple or anything. We just like to hang out and stuff."

"Yeah, stuff." Hayden held his stomach as he laughed.

I glared at him. Brother or not, the kid was losing a limb.

My mom's face lit up with excitement. "Oh, honey, I have an idea. Why don't you invite her over for dinner tonight? Your father and I would love to meet her."

I rubbed my neck. "Yeah, um...maybe next time. Clare's dad isn't home very much, so she stayed at campus for break."

My mom's face fell. "Oh, that's such a shame. I hate that she's alone for Thanksgiving. That's got to be awfully lonely."

"Yeah, I suppose. Some other students were also staying over break, so she won't be alone." It gave me comfort knowing that Kitty and Todd would keep her company. The muscles in my body immediately tensed when I thought about who else in that group

118

would be spending time with her...alone.

Fucking Paul.

I gritted my teeth. Just thinking about that guy being near her made my blood boil. She spent more time with him than anyone, and I hated it. Clare had to be blind not to see how badly he wanted her. I could see it in his eyes every time I caught him walking her home after class. The fact she considered him one of her best friends didn't make that any easier.

Maybe she didn't see him as a threat, but I sure as hell did. As long as Clark Kent kept his hands off her, he'd live to see another day.

"Eric, I don't want that poor girl staying there for Christmas. Do you understand? Drag her home with you, if you have to. She's welcome to spend the holidays with us."

I pushed thoughts of Paul away and chuckled at how worked up my mom was getting. "I will, Mom."

The idea of Clare sitting around the tree with our family on Christmas morning absolutely thrilled me. Then again, everything about Clare Winston thrilled me.

I'd been teasing her to not fall for someone else while I was gone. But the truth was, I had fallen head over heels in love with her a long time ago. I just didn't know how to come out and tell her, especially since I'd been the one to urge her to explore her options.

A loud horn blared outside, causing my dad to let out a loud curse.

"That's Travis." I yanked a sweatshirt over my head. "Coach Parton's supposed to let us onto the high school field so we can throw the ball around for a while."

"Just don't be late for dinner. I'm making your favorite lasagna.

Tell Travis he's welcome to join us."

"Yes, ma'am." I gave my mom a kiss on the cheek and headed out the door, eager to get my feet back on my home field.

◆ ◆ ◆ ◆

Sweat stung my eyes as I waited for Travis's tall figure to get to the right position. When he neared the right spot and looked my way, I extended my arm and launched a long pass to him. Jumping into the air, he caught the leather ball with perfect ease. I clapped my hands in celebration. When it came to playing football, we were a force to be reckoned with, always in sync with each other.

Exhausted from our workout, I waved him in. My right shoulder was killing me, and with training starting back up after break, I didn't need to overwork it.

"It sure is good seeing you two back on this field," Coach Parton said as he tossed us each a cold bottle of water.

"It's good to be back." I glanced across the stadium, reminiscing. My time at Ridgeville High would always hold a special place in my heart. Who knows, maybe one day I would find myself coaching here.

After finishing off our drinks, Travis and I waited at the gate while Coach P. locked up.

"Listen, why don't the two of you come over to the house tomorrow and catch the game? We've got a seventy-two-inch projection screen downstairs now."

"Sweet! Count me in," I said.

Hanging at Coach P.'s house was always a blast. Of course, it didn't hurt that his wife was also hot as hell. Practically every guy on our team fantasized about her. I knew I certainly had.

Travis cleared his throat. "Sorry, I'll have to pass. I've got plans tomorrow afternoon."

I snapped my head toward him. "With who? Your fist?" I joked. This was the first I'd heard about any plans. If he was blowing off watching football for a girl, it must be serious.

Travis threw his bag at me, a hint of embarrassment filling his face. "No, asshole. If you must know, I'm going to the movies with Tori."

Although my best friend would never come out and admit it, he'd had a thing for Tori Belman since we were freshmen in high school. Travis could snap his fingers and make just about any girl drop their panties for him. But, for some reason, he didn't seem to want that from Tori. If I didn't know better, I might think he was in love with her. I could tease him about it, but it wasn't like I had any room to talk. My heart completely belonged to Clare, and I damn well knew it.

"All right then, it looks like it'll just be you and me, Coach."

◆ ◆ ◆ ◆

"Touchdown, baby! Whooo!" I high-fived Coach Parton and scooted toward the edge of my seat, watching the replay of the quarterback's throw.

He took a swig of his beer and pointed to the screen in front of us. "I predict that'll be you in five years."

"Me?" I snorted, nearly choking on my drink. "I don't know about that."

"I'm serious, son. You have a huge future in front of you. With your record this year, I wouldn't be surprised if scouts started approaching you pretty soon. They started on me my sophomore year." He absentmindedly rubbed his knee. A motorcycle accident his senior year of college had robbed him of a career in football. The disappointment was still evident in his eyes.

"Hey, guys. I'm sorry to interrupt."

I'd been so engrossed with the game that I hadn't noticed his wife come downstairs.

Coach P. lifted up the remote and hit the mute button. "It's fine, baby. What's up?"

Smiling, she turned her attention toward me. "Eric, I was wondering if you could come help me upstairs in the kitchen. I'm having trouble reaching something in one of our cabinets."

She and I were basically the same height, but I shrugged and stood. "Sure."

I set my cup on the table and followed her out of the room. Grabbing the handrail, I paused at the foot of the stairs and peered up, unable to ignore the view of her ass as she sauntered up the steep set of stairs.

Goddamn. Coach P. was one lucky son of a bitch.

Once we were in the kitchen she moved in front of the long row of cabinets. My eyes zoned in on the rising hem of her short dress as she stood tiptoe. She pointed at the top shelf.

"It's that one, right there."

Just as I stepped behind her, she pushed her ass back against me, rotating her hips until I could feel my cock hardening. Shocked by her forwardness, I jumped back and away.

"What are you doing?"

A playful grin spread across her beautiful face. "Oh, come on,

Eric. I was just having a little fun." She reached for the hem of my T-shirt, tugging me closer to her. I gasped when her other hand dropped to cup my erection.

"W-We can't do this."

"Why not?" she whispered across my lips.

Placing my hands on her shoulders, I pushed her to the side.

"Because, it's wrong, that's why. You're my coach's wife, for fuck's sake."

She threw her head back and laughed. "Do you honestly think Stephen doesn't know what we're doing up here?" She pointed up to the corner of the room where a tiny black camera was positioned in the ceiling. "Wave. He's watching us."

Staring up at the camera, I thought back to that day in Coach P.'s office when he'd walked in on me and Clare and didn't stop us. Beyond that, he'd encouraged Travis to join in, a decision I had probably spent too much time thinking about now that I was in love with Clare.

Now it all made perfect sense though. Coach Parton was a freak.

"I've got a little confession to make." Mrs. Parton teased her fingertips across my abdomen, just above the elastic waistband of my pants. "I've wanted you since the night you threw that winning touchdown." Her hand slid beneath the band, slowly inching downward. "You were dripping with sweat, so high on your win."

I let out a ragged breath when her hand wrapped around my thick girth and stroked me up and down.

"Those tight white pants were hugging your perfect ass. Right then and there, I imagined what you would taste like, how you would feel inside me." Releasing me, she eased her body down to the tile floor, tugging my pants down along with her. When my dick sprang free, her face lit up with excitement. "Mmm. Look at that beautiful cock." She eagerly licked her lips as she wrapped her hand around the base of my shaft and pumped up and down. "I always knew you'd be big."

Her strokes grew stronger, faster. It felt so good that I had to grip the sides of the countertop to support myself.

"You've. Got. To. Stop." I panted through each word.

Dropping her head, she licked her way up my length, pausing at my tip to flick her tongue across the head of my cock. My body shook from the pleasure. Mrs. Parton looked up at me through hooded eyes.

"Be honest with me, Eric. Do you really want me to stop?"

Fuck no.

Just as I started to answer, she stole every rational thought I had by taking my entire length into her mouth.

"Holy fucking shit," I growled. She adjusted her position, taking me even deeper, until the tip of my cock hit the back of her throat. I dropped my head back, savoring the feel of her hot velvet mouth as my dick slid back and forth between her lips. Each slide brought me closer and closer to blowing my load in her mouth.

"Whoa. Stop," I said.

A loud pop echoed across the kitchen as she broke the tight seal around my cock. I sank back against the counter and tried to catch my breath.

Wearing a wide, satisfied grin, Mrs. Parton hoisted herself up onto the counter across from me, and then slowly spread her legs. She traced her fingertips over the thin piece of material that covered her pussy.

"Have you ever been with an older woman, Eric?" She tugged the material to the side, circling her fingers into the moisture of her folds.

I licked my lips and shook my head.

"No."

"Then, you've been missing out."

She tugged the jersey dress over her head, revealing a skimpy red bra and panties. Instantly, my eyes heated with desire, devouring every inch as they roamed her glorious body. Even at thirty-eight, Mrs. Parton could put any swimsuit model to shame.

She grabbed my hand and brought it to her opening. I moaned when I felt the heat of her soaked cunt.

"Mmm, that's right. Feel how wet I am for you."

I shoved two fingers into her and groaned when her eyes flared with desire. "Does this greedy little pussy want me?"

"God, yes! Fuck me, Eric. Show me what that young cock can do. Make me scream."

Retrieving my fingers, I glanced down at the beautiful ripe pussy in front of me and swallowed hard. She would be different than any other woman I'd been with. She was someone who knew exactly what she wanted and what it took to get it. How could I pass up the chance to see how it would be with someone with this much sexual experience and confidence?

Before I could blink, she was ripping a condom wrapper with her teeth. I took a deep breath, savoring the feel of her hand as she rolled the latex down my length.

In one swift move, I scooped an arm beneath each of her knees and lifted her up into position. As I thrusted my pelvis forward, my long cock disappeared inch by inch between the lips of her pussy. The searing heat of her inner walls penetrated through the thin layer of latex, unraveling my control. My steady movements grew wild and feral.

Without pulling myself out, I slid my hands beneath her, cupping her ass as I lifted her up off the counter. We didn't miss a beat. I bounced her up and down on my length, her cunt squeezing against my forceful thrusts. The death grip she had around my cock told me she was close.

"God, you're so fucking big. I'm going to come!" Shuddering, she stilled to ride out her orgasm.

I was relentless, pumping myself in and out of her pussy, determined to give her what she wanted.

"You wanted to scream my name? Then, fucking scream it," I growled, slamming her back against the wall behind her, inadvertently knocking a picture onto the floor.

"Oh. My. God. Eric! Yes! Give it to me harder!"

I let out a loud growl, ramming into her body like some wild beast. She crashed her lips to mine, plunging her tongue into my mouth as her hands dug into my hair. The heaviness in my balls was too much for me to hold back.

I pulled out of her, yanked off the condom, and fisted my cock in my hand.

Mrs. Parton dropped to her knees in front of me. Looking up at me, she opened her mouth, inviting my come.

The powerful orgasm stole my breath. I squeezed the base of my cock and came on her waiting lips. Mrs. Parton surprised me by guiding me into her mouth. She slid down my length a few times, and then released me.

"Fucking delicious," she rasped, jolting me out of my blissful haze.

The gravity of what had just happened hit me all at once. Clare's sweet face came to mind. I ran my hands through my hair.

"Jesus! What did I just do?"

"You just fucked my wife," Coach Parton's voice came from behind me. I jerked my pants up and spun around to face him, unsure how he was going to react to all of this.

"Coach, I—"

He held up his hand and walked over to his wife.

She flashed me a wicked grin before turning around and gripping the sides of the wooden breakfast table.

"Thanks for getting her ready for me, Hayward." Unashamed, he dropped his pants right in front of me, situated himself behind his wife's perched ass, and gave her a few hard slaps across her backside. He shoved his cock into her, glancing over his shoulder at me mid-thrust.

"You're welcome to stay and watch, son. She loves an audience."

"I-I've got to go." I barreled toward the front door and did not stop until I reached my Jeep. I fought to keep my shaking hands steady enough to put the keys in the ignition. Throwing it in reverse, I slammed my foot on the accelerator, squealing my tires as I backed out of the driveway.

Once I was on the main highway, I angrily slammed my hand down on the steering wheel. "You're such a fucking idiot!" I screamed.

Suddenly, my phone lit up in my cup holder, illuminating the dark cab of the Jeep.

Guilt rushed over me when I read Clare's name on the screen. I took a deep breath and answered the call, silently praying she wouldn't be able to hear the shame in my voice.

"Hey, beautiful. Are you calling to tell me you've fallen for someone?"

I was hoping the joke would lighten my mood. Clare's laugh made everything melt away. She was like the warmest sunshine on the coldest, darkest day.

"Maybe I am."

Like a lovesick fool, I grinned into the phone. "Oh, really? Tell me who he is so I can kick his ass when I get back."

"He's this star quarterback. I don't know if you know him or not."

"He sounds like a prick."

She giggled into the phone. "Yeah, sometimes he can be."

"Hmm, is that so? Well, tell me, does he know how you feel about him?" I held my breath as I waited for her to answer.

"I don't know, but I'm hoping he figures it out really soon."

The deafening silence on the phone made my heart ache. I hated that I couldn't have her in my arms, that I couldn't feel her against me.

"I miss you, Eric." The intensity in her voice shook me to the core. I looked at the green exit sign up ahead. Four hours and I could be back with her. Putting on my signal, I turned onto the exit ramp and merged onto the interstate. My parents would be furious, but they'd get over it. I had a girl to get back to.

"I'll be there soon, baby. Don't worry."

CHAPTER NINE

CLARE

I read over the highlighted paragraph in my Abnormal Psychology textbook for the fourth time, but the words wouldn't stick. I couldn't get Eric's voice out of my head. He'd sounded like his same charming self over the phone, but something felt off. I hung up the phone after our call and cried into my pillow, hating our physical distance as much as I was growing to hate the way other people were coming between us all the time.

Still, he'd all but mandated that I experiment and push my boundaries while at school. Without a doubt, I was enjoying my various encounters and discovering things about my sexuality that I never thought I would. Last night with Paul was earth-shattering in its own right, even if I was worried my friend cared about the emotional piece of our union more than he let on.

But no matter what I did, no matter who I let into my body, I couldn't shake the way I felt about Eric. I loved him—truly, completely. I'd wanted him so badly and for so long that I wasn't sure I'd ever be able to get him out of my heart. Worse, I knew deep down he wanted to be there. But how could we have a future this way?

A knock at the door pulled me from my troubled thoughts. I rose from my desk and opened the door to find Paul balancing a pizza box on his palm.

He lifted it up with a smirk. "Hungry?"

"Of course."

I smiled warmly, because Paul had that effect on me. I didn't deny relishing our time together, the same way I didn't regret the easy friendship that had formed between us these first few months of school. I moved aside and let him inside my dorm room. He set the box at the edge of the desk and peered over my textbook.

"Homework? On holiday break?" He lifted an eyebrow, gracing me with another amused look. His eyes were kind behind his glasses.

My heart twisted with affection. I tried to ignore the way I craved his touch, too, in that moment. Instead, I nudged him away playfully and dropped down into my chair. "You're one to talk, book nerd."

He sat on the bed, and we each took a piece of pizza. We chewed in silence, but the air was thick with tension. Mostly sexual tension, I figured, based on the way his gaze traveled over my bare legs to where my university shorts hit the tops of my thighs.

I'd been moping around in my room all day and hadn't bothered changing into real clothes. I'd been too busy replaying our night together over and over in my head. Paul and I had shared something special, but I couldn't ignore the uneasiness I now felt.

"Are you okay?"

I widened my eyes and looked up. His gaze was thoughtful, like he was worried for me.

I nodded with a swallow. "I'm fine. Just, you know, getting

my head back in the game for Monday when classes start back up. Finals are right around the corner, and I'm hoping to stay ahead of the stress."

He stared down at his feet. "That's not really what I mean."

A few seconds passed before I spoke again. "You mean last night?"

Our eyes locked, and he nodded.

"I'm fine, Paul, really. I had fun. I hope you did too."

He bit his lip and averted his eyes again. Instinctively, I wanted to know what my friend was thinking, but another part of me was scared to ask.

"Who is he? Who is this guy who has your heart?"

My breath rushed out. "Paul..."

"No, I want to know who puts that look on your face. I see it tonight, and I've seen it before. I can make you happier than he does, I know it."

"You don't understand. It's complicated."

He frowned and his jaw tightened. "I'd never share you, Clare. I'd cherish you. Every minute you gave to me, every touch. I'd never take it for granted."

My head fell into my hands, and I fought back tears. He couldn't know what this kind of agony was like...

He took my hand and pulled me to him. I thought about resisting, but I wanted the comfort of his arms as they folded around me. We sat that way for a long time, his strong arms cradling me tightly, my body nestled against him, and my thighs straddling his. No matter what happened between us, I cared for Paul and I cherished his friendship. Maybe sleeping together had been a mistake, but his affection was a gift I wasn't going to squander.

"Thank you for everything you've given me, Paul," I whispered, trying like hell to keep my emotions in check.

He pulled back so he could look into my eyes. His deep green gaze seemed to reach into my soul. "You're thanking me?"

"I'm sorry, Paul. You promised me..." A tear fell down my cheek. "You promised nothing would change."

He caught my cheek and silenced me with a timid kiss. I kissed him back, tightening my grasp around him as our tongues met and dueled passionately. He pulled away breathless, touching me with restless hands.

"Clare, I promised you that nothing would change. I loved you before, and I could only love you more after what we did. I'll accept whatever you give me, but goddamn, you can't stop me from trying to give you everything you deserve. You deserve the world. Love. Devotion."

"Paul..." I wanted to beg his forgiveness. I couldn't give him what he wanted. Heaven help me, I wished I could...

Could I?

He hushed me with another deep kiss, and we moved to my bed. There was nothing tentative about the way he touched me. His kisses were hungry and consuming, like he was trying to communicate every intense emotion with the flicks of his tongue and the way he yanked at my clothing. My own emotions rioted. My love for Eric. My affection for Paul. The primal needs of my body. Everything mixed, creating a tornado of feeling and a fierce need to release all of it.

Paul tugged off his shirt, and then pulled down my shorts and panties. He buried his face between my thighs. I cried out and threaded my fingers through his dark, silky locks. He licked and sucked, and I guided his motions, rotating my hips against his full lips and eager tongue.

"Put your fingers inside me," I whimpered. "Fuck me deep, Paul. Please...I need to feel you."

He slipped two fingers into me, fucking and twisting, bringing me to the brink while his mouth never stopped. He cursed, murmured my name, promised me everything I wanted against my pulsing, wet flesh. I didn't have to reach for it. The orgasm ripped through me. I screamed and tightened my grip on Paul as I flew into the intense feeling.

In that moment, everything was right, in sync. The bliss was temporary, though. A loud crash jolted me. Paul's fingers slipped from me as he straightened.

And Eric's frame hovered at the edge of the room.

ERIC

"What are you doing here?" Clare scrambled to a sitting position, dragging a blanket to cover the lower half of her body.

"What the fuck are *you* doing here?" I snapped at her, accusation thick in my tone. I knew I had no right to say the words, but I couldn't help the way they flew from my lips.

Paul had been posted up between her beautiful thighs, his lips glossy with her arousal. A low growl tore from my chest, and I tightened my fists.

"You. Get out." I pointed toward the door.

Paul drew his dark brows together. Slowly, he grabbed his T-shirt off the floor and pulled it on. He rose and faced me squarely, almost threateningly.

"You don't deserve her." His tone was quiet, barely a whisper, but unmistakably serious.

I couldn't conjure up a reply before he slipped past me and through Clare's busted door. Maybe because deep down I believed him. How could I possibly deserve Clare...after everything I'd done? A flash of fucking Coach P.'s wife penetrated my thoughts, and a wave of nausea hit me.

Yet, as I'd heard Clare's scream of ecstasy on the other side of that door, I couldn't help myself. Nothing could have kept me from her. Nothing, and no one.

Paul. I fucking knew it. I knew he wanted her. The way he looked at her spoke of an underlying affection that made my skin crawl with jealousy.

I had no right to feel it. But Jesus Christ, I'd talked to her hours earlier. How could she do this when she knew I was on my way to her?

Clare shifted over the bed and pulled on her shorts. When she came to me, tears glimmered in her eyes.

"Why are you here?"

"I hung up with you and was on my way here. And this is what I walk in on?"

"What you walk in on?" Her voice was loud and shaky with emotion. "You broke my fucking door!"

"Did you fuck him?" I had to know. I just had to know.

Her jaw was tight and she took another step toward me. She was without makeup, but her cheeks were flushed. She was gorgeous, and I had to restrain myself from pulling her to me and fucking her senseless. I didn't care where Paul had been or what they'd done. Goddamnit, she was mine.

"Yes," she said calmly. "I slept with him. He cares about me, and I care about him. We're friends."

I shook my head, filled with fresh rage.

"You did this," she whispered, tears brimming her eyes. "You pushed me away. You wanted it this way. And so this is who I am, because I can't have you the way I want to."

I closed my eyes. "Clare...baby."

"Get out."

My eyes flew open. "What?"

"Just get out."

I closed the small space between us. Determination burned like fire in my veins. "No."

She tried to hold her ground, but took an unsteady step back. "Eric."

I caught her wrist and pulled her toward me. "You can get pissed. You can hate me, resent me. You can fuck your friends and drive me out of my goddamn mind. But you've always been mine and you always will be."

"How can you say that?" She shook her head, avoiding my penetrating gaze.

"Because I love you. And I've never loved anyone. I loved you enough to let you go, to let you feel things and have experiences that rip my heart out."

"I think you should go." Her voice lacked the punch it had

earlier.

I looped my arm around her waist and hauled her against me. "Maybe Paul's right. I may not deserve you, but that doesn't change the fact that I can't breathe without you."

Crashing my lips against hers, I released something between a sigh and a moan because she was in my arms again. Four hours on the road and I'd entertained every fantasy of claiming her body, fucking her until she screamed my name into the air. I could have never expected this would go down. But as angry as she was, she melted against me now. Her hands twined around my neck as I kissed her deeper.

"Say you're mine, Clare."

I nibbled along her jaw, sucking her neck until she gasped.

"I'm yours, Eric. I've always been yours."

"Good. Now I'm going to show you."

I turned her abruptly, kicked her chair away, and bent her over the desk. Her hands scrambled over the books and notes that littered the surface. Yanking her shorts down, I revealed her perfect bare ass and glistening pussy. My jaw clenched, because I knew Paul had already made her come. I had to mark her...show her that she was truly mine over anyone else.

"Did he fuck you bare?"

"No!" The anger was back in her voice, along with a twinge of guilt.

"Good. Because I'm about to."

Her fingers curled over the edge of the wood desk, her ass perched high in the air like she was waiting for me, saying yes to me.

Thank God, because this was what I needed. Just her and me.

Nothing between us. I pushed up her shirt and worked my zipper down to free my cock. I was beyond hard. I teased the tip up and down her slick pussy. A small whimper escaped her lips, which morphed into a guttural moan when I shoved into her with one fierce thrust. My eyes rolled back. Nothing on God's green earth had ever felt better than the warm, wet haven of her pussy.

"Yes!" she screamed as I fucked her hard and fast.

No way could I go slow. Not now.

Almost instantly, her pussy became a tight fist around me, like her body was demanding my come. "Going to come in you, baby."

"I want you to," she mewled.

I hooked my arm behind her elbows and arched her back to me so I could reach her neck and murmur in her ear as I took those last strokes inside her.

"No one's ever going to come in you but me, Clare. Understand?"

"Yes."

"And when he puts his mouth on you, when he shoves his cock in you, he'll know this pussy is mine."

I bit down on her shoulder and her whole body began to shake and spasm, forcing the orgasm to rush over me. A long groan left me as I pumped hard and deep into the beautiful woman who'd completely ravaged my heart.

CLARE

My muscles went lax under the warm shower, but I still felt shaky from Eric's violent fucking. He lathered my loofa and washed over my shoulders, down my back, and gently between my legs. Moments ago, as I was floating down from the intense high of my orgasm, Eric's release dripping warm down my thighs, I had felt very much his. He owned my body and I never wanted that to change, even if I had to figure out how to live without exclusivity.

He kissed my shoulder and held his body flush against me.

"I love you," he murmured.

I melted a little bit more. I turned in his arms and slid my fingers through his damp hair. I remembered the first time he kissed me. His hair had been dark and damp from sweat, and somehow, after years of me silently adoring him, he finally saw me. Now, he was here, in my heart.

"Why did you come back to me?"

He winced but his lips stayed tight. A familiar flash of jealousy burned through me.

"Did you see Mandy?"

His frown deepened. "No. I told you, I'm done with her."

I relaxed, glad to know that catty bitch didn't get her claws into my man. But tension lingered in Eric's body as he held me.

"What happened?"

He shook his head with a sigh. "I was at Coach's house watching a game, and his wife...she came onto me. I don't know. It was fucked up."

My eyes widened. "She cheated on him?"

"No, it wasn't like that. It's going to sound weird, but I think it was kind of like foreplay for them. He started going at her right afterward. I got the hell out of there and called you. Then I knew I couldn't wait anymore to be with you. I should have never left you here by yourself."

I sighed, not liking the story he told me, but feeling grateful for his honesty. Apparently we'd each had our own misadventures. I just wasn't sure how much longer we could keep this up.

"Eric..."

He lowered his head, brushing his lips sweetly across mine. My thoughts scattered when he hitched my thigh over his hip and slid his cock into me slowly.

"What, baby?" His voice was a quiet rasp, reminding me that we were still having a conversation.

"Eric...how can we keep doing this? I don't want to hurt you anymore."

He thrust again and pleasure rippled through me. "We'll always have this. Just you and me. No matter what happens, if we have this"—he held me tighter and rooted in the deepest part of me, sending a shockwave through my core—"we'll always find our way back to each other."

The next few strokes rendered me speechless. We'd have to figure it all out another day. Because he was right. With every thick stroke, every greedy touch, every promise uttered in the climb toward ecstasy, we were finding our way back to each other.

CHAPTER TEN

CLARE

"Clare! Wait up!"

I froze at the sound of Paul's voice. For the past two days, I had successfully managed to avoid him by skipping all of our mutual classes. I knew it was cowardly, but I still couldn't bring myself to face him, especially after what had happened between us the other night.

Tightening my hold on my bag, I darted toward the nearest exit of the building and picked up my pace in an effort to ditch him. I had just reached the stairwell when he grabbed my arm. Stiffening my body, I refused to turn around to look at him.

"Let me go, Paul."

"Clare, please. Look at me," he pleaded, keeping a firm grip around my wrist.

I hesitantly faced him. "I said 'let me go.' I don't want to do this with you right now."

He looked at me for a few seconds before reluctantly releasing me. "Fine. Then, meet me tonight. We need to talk about everything, Clare. You at least owe me that much."

I shook my head. "I don't owe you anything, Paul. I told you from the beginning not to expect anything from me. What happened between us was just sex. It didn't mean anything."

"Well, it meant something to me." He swallowed hard, reaching his hand out to cup my face. "I meant what I said before. I love you, Clare."

Shaking my head, I stumbled backward. "You can't love me, Paul. We're just friends... Friends with benefits."

Paul's shoulders sagged. "I've been in love with you since the moment Kitty and Todd introduced us at the campus bonfire. I tried hinting that I was interested, but you never seemed to notice. You were too wrapped up with Eric to see it. I tried to be patient. I tried to convince myself that you were worth waiting for. But the more time that went by, the more I began to give up hope that you would ever see me as more than just a friend. Then, that night over Thanksgiving break happened. Since then, you're all I fucking think about. I can still taste your pussy on my lips. I can still remember how incredible it felt to be inside you. Please, I'm begging you, Clare. Just give me tonight. Let me prove to you that I can be what you need."

A wave of nausea swept through my body. No, no, no! This wasn't the way it was supposed to happen.

"Paul, I'm in love with Eric. I know how fucked up that must seem to you, especially after we were together, but it's true. No matter what happened between us, what I feel for him is never going to change." At least, I didn't think it would.

An agonized look washed over his face. "How can you honestly say you love him, Clare? I would cherish you. Love you. Just give me a chance, please. I can make you forget about him." Before I could open my mouth to speak, Paul stepped forward and grabbed me by the waist, planting a passionate kiss on my lips. I clamped my lips together, refusing him entry into my mouth. Desperate to break the kiss, I placed my hands on his chest and shoved him away from me.

"What the fuck?" I brought my hand up to my mouth, glaring back at him, my chest heaving as I fought to catch my breath.

Paul ran his hands through his hair, tugging at the ends. Regret filled his eyes. "God, Clare. I'm so sorry. It's just... All of this is just making me so crazy."

He wasn't the only one. Things with Eric were confusing enough as it was. I felt like everything was closing in around me. Paul's professed love was the last thing I needed to deal with right now.

"Look, Paul, this is all getting way out of control. Maybe it's best if we keep our distance from each other for a while. I need some time to make sense of everything."

Paul flinched, as if my words had somehow gutted him. Swallowing hard, he nodded his head. "If that's what you want, I'm willing to give you all the space you need. I'll be here when you're ready to talk."

"Thank you."

Despite the present drama, Paul really was a terrific guy. I regretted crossing that dangerous line in our friendship—a line we could never cross back over. I was finding out there were a lot of terrific guys out there. Sexy, intelligent, caring men who could make both my body and my heart respond.

As I thought back over the last couple of months and the outrageous agreement Eric and I had reached, on the one hand, I felt empowered. I'd had experiences and fun. But with the sex came the emotional side, and not just with Paul. It was becoming tougher to keep this simple, to keep the questions at bay. I'd hurt Paul even though I'd been clear. Did Eric deserve the parts of myself I was holding out just for him? Was this arrangement with Eric worth all the pain that seemed to go along with it? Could someone like Paul... or Reed...be more if I gave either of them that chance?

Reed Michaels.

The sexy surfer was far more than an island hookup. He had made me feel things that I had never experienced with anyone. The deep connection we had shared was unexplainable and far more than passionate sex. If I was honest with myself, it was probably a good thing that four thousand miles separated me from Reed.

I dug out my phone from my bag and scrolled through my contacts, smiling weakly at Reed's name on the screen. For what must have been the hundredth time since I left Kauai, I fought with myself over whether to press the green button that would make the call connecting me to Reed.

Maybe if I heard his voice I could make sense of everything. Maybe he was the key to figuring my way through this fucked-up place I'd put myself in. But like so many times before, I chickened out on calling him. I tucked the phone back into the side pocket of my bag, believing that I'd made the right decision to keep that part of my past in the past.

◆ ◆ ◆ ◆

The loud tolling of the bell on the campus clock tower broke me from my trance. Fluttering my eyes, I noticed the evening sky around me.

I had convinced myself that I could clear my head with a walk, but obviously I hadn't thought things through. Not only was I on the far end of campus, I was also wearing the wrong kind of shoes. I winced at the pain in each step, knowing I still had a long walk back. The heels of my feet might never forgive me for this mistake.

By the time I made it to my dorm, every inch of my body was aching from fatigue. All I wanted was to take a hot shower and climb into bed. Maybe I would be able to see things more clearly after a good night's sleep.

Just as I was about to pull out my keys to my room, Eric's familiar ringtone sounded from the side pocket of my bag. Ordinarily, I would jump at the chance to hear his voice, but my run-in with Paul had simply pushed me over the edge. Between the two of them, I felt like a ping pong ball being hit back and forth. All of it was sucking the life out of me. Digging out my phone, I cringed and sent the call to voicemail. Maybe ignoring him like this was wrong, but it seemed like the only feasible solution at the moment.

Lacey was toweling off her long hair when I entered our room. When she saw my disheveled appearance, her mouth dropped open. "Holy shit! What happened to you? You look like hell."

Exhausted, I dropped my bag by the door and collapsed across my mattress, deciding to skip the shower and go straight to bed.

"Can we talk about it tomorrow, please?" I mumbled into my pillow. The sooner I went to sleep, the sooner I could forget about everything.

There was a shuffling noise beside me, followed by a hard kick against my bed. Cursing, I pushed myself off the bed and glared at my roommate, who was towering over me.

"Don't you listen?"

Lacey nudged me with her hip. "Shut up and scoot over."

As I shifted myself over on the bed, I eyed the tall bottle in her right hand. "What's that?" She let out a low chuckle. "Meet José Cuervo. Your new best friend."

ERIC

"Hey, this is Clare. Sorry I missed your call..."

I didn't bother leaving another message. I'd left four. There were at least a hundred rational reasons why she wasn't answering, but none of them settled the uneasiness that resided inside me. Something wasn't right. I could feel it.

"Hayward! Stop dicking around and get your ass on that field!" My coach's angry voice resonated through the empty locker room. With the end of our football season approaching, I knew how important these practices were. If we secured these last two wins, we would be headed to conference playoffs—an accomplishment this school had not seen in years. No matter how messed up my head was, I had to get my shit together. I couldn't let my team down.

"Yes, sir!" I tossed my phone back onto my bag and grabbed my helmet from the bench. Hustling past my coach, I made my way out of the field house.

For the next hour, I'd give it my all, but the second practice was over, I was heading to Clare's room. One way or another, I would know the reason for her silence.

CLARE

"Oh, my God! I have the best idea!" Lacey bolted upright in her bed.

Laughing, I reached for the bottle and poured myself another drink. "What's this brilliant idea?" I happened to think the tequila was the best idea she'd had in a long time. After everything that had happened today, this was exactly what I needed to take the edge off.

"Let's play *Truth or Dare*."

I frowned and set my glass down. "Uh-uh. No way. I hate that game."

Lacey turned to face me, hugging a pillow against her stomach. "Oh, come on. It'll be fun. We'll just play one round. If you don't like it, we'll stop."

I shook my head. "No."

"Pleeaasse," she whined.

God, I fucking hated when she begged like that. Having a few drinks in her made it even worse.

"Fine, but just one round," I warned. Surely I had enough liquid courage flowing through my veins to make it through one round of this game.

Lacey beamed. "I'll even let you go first," she offered, rubbing her hands together excitedly.

Rolling my eyes, I started off the game. "Okay, truth or dare?"

"Truth." She grinned, wiggling her eyebrows at me. "Better make this question a good one."

That was easy. I'd been dying to know about something for months.

"So...is it true that the dorm janitor caught you handcuffed in the basement with Brent Morrison on Halloween?"

Without delay, Lacey leaned forward and opened her nightstand drawer. When she held up her hand, a set of shiny metal handcuffs dangled from her fingertips. "Yep. And it was totally worth getting caught. The things that boy can do with his tongue..."

We busted out laughing. God, it felt so good to laugh. Maybe this game wasn't so bad after all.

"My turn," Lacey announced, clearing her throat. "Truth or dare?"

"Truth," I answered, holding my breath as I awaited her question. Judging from the mischievous look on her face, I knew I was in for it.

"How did you *really* get your grade up so fast in Human Sexuality?"

Fuck, this was exactly why I hated this game. I looked her straight in the eye and answered the best way I could, without actually getting into the details.

"I already told you. Extra credit."

The pillow Lacey had been hugging came flying across the room, smacking me in the head. "You little liar! Okay, now you have to do the dare."

"What? No way! I told you the truth," I protested.

Lacey shrugged. "It doesn't matter. I don't believe you, so that means you still have to do my dare."

Shit. Maybe I should just tell her what really happened with Professor Drake, especially since he'd taken a permanent position at another college two weeks after our encounter. Still, if what happened ever got out, I would lose my scholarship. I simply couldn't risk that happening, especially given my financial situation.

I crossed my arms, cringing inwardly at what she had up her sleeve. "What's the dare?"

No matter what she said, I wasn't running naked down the hallways.

Lacey tossed the handcuffs beside me on the bed. "Now that you know about my sexy encounter in the basement, I dare you to tell me your wildest sexual fantasy."

My shoulders tensed. I'd never told anyone my wildest fantasy, not even Eric, even though he'd inspired it. Closing my eyes, I clutched the handcuffs in my hand. The alcohol flowing through my bloodstream erased my inhibitions, helping the raunchy confession roll off my tongue.

"It's late at night, and I'm on the football field with Eric. He's wearing his jersey. He ties me to the goalpost, naked, while two other players join us. Their hands and mouths are all over me. They take me, one by one, until I'm begging for them to fill me up. When we're done, Eric takes me back to the showers for a private round."

I opened my eyes, catching the wide smirk on Lacey's face. It was then I saw she was holding up my phone.

Lacey ended the call and glanced back up at me. "What? Eric was calling your phone. I didn't want to be rude and stop you in the middle of a dare. Besides, you probably made the boy come in his pants. Who knew you were such a dirty girl?"

I narrowed my eyes at her. "You are *so* dead."

The sudden knock on our door sent a wave of panic through me.

"Don't let him in yet. I look like hell," I warned, trying to smooth back my tangled hair. I had barely stood from the bed before Lacey was opening the door to our room.

"Hey, Eric. Come on in."

I nervously turned my head, our eyes locking instantly. Eric was drenched in sweat. He looked like he had come straight from the gym. We stared at each other for what seemed like forever, until Lacey broke the awkward silence that filled the room.

"You know what? I think I'm gonna go crash in Tatum and Katie's room tonight," she announced as she grabbed the near-empty bottle of tequila from the table and slipped it beneath her shirt to conceal it. "Don't do anything I wouldn't do," Lacey sang as she closed the door behind her.

Eric eyed me cautiously from across the room. The concern on his face was evident.

"Are you avoiding me for some reason? I've been trying to reach you all day."

I dropped onto my bed, unsure of how to answer him. "I'm sorry. I've just had a lot on my mind."

Eric pulled out my chair and took my hands in his. "Talk to me, Clare. Don't push me away."

I sighed. "I think I ruined my friendship with Paul. You probably don't want to hear about this though."

"He loves you," he muttered, his expression tight.

I shrugged because I couldn't lie. Paul had told me as much.

"But I don't love him. I love you."

He released a sigh. "But you care about him. It doesn't take long for those feelings to deepen, believe me." He placed his hand on my chest. "Anyone who holds a part of your heart keeps you from fully giving it to me. I want all of it, Clare. I won't share it with anyone."

I lifted my gaze to his, fresh hope breaking through my malaise. "What are you saying?"

"I'm saying that you were right. We can't keep doing this for much longer. I already know what I want. I just need to know that's what you want too."

I shook my head quickly, but it only made me dizzy. "Eric. No, that's what I want too. I just want to be with you. No one else."

He brushed my hair back and tucked it behind my ear. "You've got three weeks, Clare. Three weeks to face your desires and decide if you're willing to give everything and everyone else up for me, and only me. Come Christmas, we either commit to each other completely, or we walk away from each other forever."

A feeling of panic washed over me. "But I don't want to lose you."

"You haven't lost me, Clare. I just need to know without a doubt that it's only us you want." Eric pressed a kiss to my forehead. "We'll talk about it later."

Full of desperation, I grabbed him by his shirt. "No, please don't leave me. Just stay with me tonight."

He frowned. "That's not a good idea, baby. Between the alcohol and our talk, you're too vulnerable. As much as I want you, I'm not going to take advantage of you like this."

"We don't have to do anything. Just hold me until I fall asleep. Please," I pleaded.

Eric reluctantly took my hand and tugged his shirt over his head, leaving his shorts on as he crawled into my bed. I pulled the covers up over us and scooted toward him, slipping into that perfect little nook. He gently stroked my hair with his fingertips. Soon, the rhythmic beat of his heart began to lull me to sleep. In those beautiful moments before I slipped away into slumber, I savored the feel of what forever could be like with Eric.

ERIC

Where the fuck are you?

I hit send on the text and set my phone down on the table as I waited for Travis's reply—not that I expected one anytime soon. He was already over an hour late as it was. I was beginning to wonder if he was even going to show up.

Bracing my elbows on the table, I raked my hands through my hair. No matter how hard I tried, I couldn't stop thinking about Clare's fantasy. The fact it involved me made it even more important, especially since we now had a deadline on this open relationship. As much as it hurt to think about sharing her with other guys, losing her would hurt more. Maybe by giving her this fantasy, I could somehow prove to her that I would do anything for her, even if it meant sacrificing my heart in the process.

My thoughts were interrupted when the waitress arrived with my order. "Here we are. A number three special with cheese. Can I get you anything else, sweetie?" She set the large plate of food in front of me.

I held up my hand. "No, thanks. I'm good."

"Just let me know if I can get you anything." The older lady patted me on the shoulder before moving to check on her other customers.

The double cheeseburger and fries on my plate looked delicious, but I wasn't the least bit hungry. I'd only ordered it because I felt guilty holding up a table in her section while I waited on Travis's slow ass. I swore the boy would be late to his own funeral.

I was checking my phone when Travis slid into the seat across from me. "Sorry I'm late, dude. I had to give Lucas a lift into town." He eyed my plate. "You gonna eat that?"

Shaking my head, I slid the food across the table. "Help yourself."

"Thanks, I'm starved."

He wolfed down the thick double cheeseburger in three bites. I'd never seen anything like him. He was like a human vacuum cleaner.

"So, what's up?" He grabbed a mouthful of fries.

Taking a deep breath, I leaned into the table, checking to make sure no one was listening around us. "First, I need to know I can trust you."

Travis narrowed his eyes at me, pushing the now empty plate to the side. "Of course you can trust me. I'm your best friend."

"I know that, but what I'm about to ask of you involves some pretty deep shit."

Travis looked over his shoulder and then leaned in, dropping his voice. "What's going on, Eric? Are you in some sort of trouble?"

I shook my head. "No, no, it's nothing like that. It's about Clare."

"Clare?"

I nodded and cleared my throat. "I'm planning on surprising her with something, and I need your help to pull it off."

A look of relief washed over him as he relaxed back against the back of the booth. "Shit, dude. You had me scared there for a minute. I thought you were going to ask me to help you bury a body or something." He laughed before continuing. "So what do I need to do?"

I shifted nervously in my seat. "Well, that's just it. You're part of the surprise."

"Me?" Travis snorted. "You want me to jump out of a cake naked or something?" He wiggled his eyebrows suggestively.

This conversation was getting way off track. I had to reel it in quick.

"Do you remember our threesome in Coach's office?"

Travis shot up in his seat and looked around us. "Keep your voice down. Of course I remember. How the hell do you think I could forget about something like that?"

"Apparently, Clare's been thinking about it a lot lately. I overheard her talking to her roommate about a fantasy of hers." Reaching in my pocket, I retrieved the set of handcuffs that I'd stolen off Clare's bed. I knew they belonged to Lacey, but I didn't think she'd mind if I borrowed them for a bit.

Travis smirked. "Nice. So she wants to make things kinky."

"Actually, it involves more than just those." I eyed the cuffs on the table. "I need another guy with us, someone we know we can trust." I had to be careful of our selection. If any of this got out, it could ruin her reputation, not to mention possibly getting us all kicked out of school.

Travis's eyes widened. "You mean like a gangbang?"

"Shhh!" I shot him a hard glare.

"Sorry, man." Travis eyed me. "Are you sure about this? It's just a fantasy, Eric. It doesn't mean you have to actually bring it to life. Besides, I thought you loved her."

"I *do* love her. That's why I'm doing this."

He blew out a breath. "Jesus. Don't you think this is a little extreme?"

"Maybe, but it's necessary." He had no idea what lengths I would go to when it came to Clare. "So, are you in or out?"

He shook his head, but his expression grew more serious. "Yeah, I'm in. I just hope you don't regret doing this."

There was no room for regrets, not now at least. "Any ideas about who we can bring in on this?"

"I don't know, man. Let me think." He rubbed the back of his neck and then straightened in his seat as one of our teammates walked through the door of the café. He motioned his head in that direction. "What about Tyler?"

Tyler Randall was probably the last person I would have picked, especially knowing how inexperienced he was with girls. He drunkenly admitted at one of our team bonfires that he'd only had one blowjob in his life. Throwing him into a gangbang would be like throwing him into a lion's den.

"I don't know, man. Don't you remember what he admitted to at the bonfire? He's still a virgin."

"That's what makes him perfect. Think about it. Not only is the dude clean, he's also transferring to the University of Florida in the spring. After Christmas break, he won't be around to run his mouth about anything."

I allowed the idea to run through my head. I had to admit, Tyler was a perfect candidate. There was just one problem.

"But how do we get him to agree to something like this?"

Travis winked as he waved Tyler over to our booth. "Just leave that part to me, my friend."

CLARE

The truth will set you free. At least, that was what I was hoping when I made the phone call to Megan. She knew me better than anyone, which was why I should have told her the whole story about Eric from the beginning. If anyone could help me wrap my brain around this, she could.

"Shit, Clare. Why would you agree to something like this?"

I blew out a breath. Not only had I expected the scolding, I deserved it.

"Because I didn't want to lose him. I love him, Megan. I thought it was the only way to have him in my life."

"I just don't get it. Eric told you he loves you. Why isn't that enough to end all of this? It doesn't make sense that he'd want to keep this ridiculous agreement going for three more weeks."

"He thinks there's some lingering desire that's holding me back from being with him."

"Well? Is there?" Megan asked.

I hesitated with my answer. Part of me was ashamed to admit it, but I'd already told her this much. I might as well come clean about everything else.

"Yeah, there are a few things. I had this connection with someone that I've never quite been able to shake."

"Who? You mean with this Paul guy?"

"No, that was just physical. This was much deeper."

"Maybe you need to meet with this guy so that you can sort through your feelings."

My shoulders sank. "I wish it were that easy, but unless you can find some way to magically transport me back to Hawaii, that's kind of impossible."

A loud gasp filled my ear. "Reed? But I thought he was just an island hookup?"

"There was something there between us that I can't explain. As much as I love Eric, I just haven't been able to shake Reed from my mind." I paused, toying with the ripped hem of my jeans. "Anyhow, it doesn't matter. It's not like I'll ever see him again anyway."

Megan remained quiet on the other end of the line.

It was a rare thing to render Megan speechless. I was about to make a joke about it when I glanced up at the large round clock that hung on the coffee shop wall. I had promised Eric I'd meet up with him.

"Shit, I'd better go. I'm late. I'll talk to you tomorrow. Thank you for listening."

"Promise me you'll be careful with all of this, okay? I just want you to be happy, whether that's with Eric or not."

"I will. Love you."

"Love you too."

I hurriedly gathered my things and shoved my phone into my pocket. The sudden buzz of my phone halted me in mid-step. Retrieving it, I read the message on the screen from Eric.

Meet me at the field house.

I shot a text to Lacey and then I sent Eric a reply.

On my way.

♦ ♦ ♦ ♦

The field house was dark when I arrived. I could've sworn Eric's text said to meet him here. Squinting my eyes, I noticed a dim light spilling out from one of the rooms at the back of the building. Hesitantly, I took a step forward.

"Eric?"

Using the flashlight on my phone to guide me, I crossed the workout room and headed toward the long hallway. Once I entered the locker room, I could hear the distant sound of water running. Eric must have decided to grab a quick shower after his workout.

As I glanced around the abandoned locker room, my eyes lit up with possibility. If we had the place all to ourselves, maybe Eric could use a bit of company.

I slipped off my shoes and quickly began disposing of my clothes, tossing them on a long wooden bench. A thick layer of steam poured from the showers, making it impossible to see anything from the doorway. Squinting, I inched forward. I finally made out the silhouette of a tall, muscular figure standing beneath the water. My heart raced with anticipation as I stepped my bare foot onto the wet ceramic floor. I couldn't wait to see the look on Eric's face.

The steam suddenly parted, and I made out a very familiar backside...Travis's. Guilt stricken, I looked away. But the temptation was too much to fight. Swallowing the lump in my throat, I allowed my gaze to follow the thick layer of soapy foam that trailed down his perfectly sculpted back, continuing downward until it coated his perfect ass.

Sweet Jesus, I never knew soap could be so erotic to watch.

Travis braced himself on the shower wall and ducked his head beneath the spray to rinse his hair. I bit my lower lip, drinking in every inch of his naked body. When he turned to the side, I caught a glimpse of his gloriously long cock.

My core clenched at the memory of how wonderful he had felt in my body. Like Eric, Travis was very well-endowed—a fact that made our threesome one I would never forget. Secretly, I longed to be deliciously stretched like that again. Maybe that was why my mind had conjured up the wild fantasy of being taken by multiple men in the first place.

I shut my eyes and shook my head, trying to blink away my dirty thoughts. When I reopened them, Travis was smiling at me and stroking his thick shaft. I was just about to turn when heat from another body blanketed me from behind. When I glanced down, I recognized Eric's hands as he slid them across my bare stomach.

"Like what you see, baby?" He pulled me back against him, pressing his erection into my bottom. I spun around in Eric's arms.

"I-I'm sorry. I thought it was you in here. I was going to surprise you."

Dressed in his football jersey and workout shorts, he stared down at me with those penetrating eyes, the ones that wielded complete control over my body. The heated expression on his face caught me off guard. Was he somehow turned on by all of this?

Eric's mouth turned up slightly as he cupped my face in his hand.

"Are you really sorry?" His seductive tone sent a shiver through me. He walked me backward until my back hit a wet body.

Travis reached for my hips and brushed his mouth against my ear as he spoke. "Don't be sorry, Clare. I'm not."

"W-What's going on?" I stuttered, nervously looking up at Eric for some sort of explanation.

Eric ran the pad of his thumb across my jaw. "As much as I want you all to myself, I think there are some things that you need to get out of your system. It's the only way to help erase those doubts in your head."

His smoldering gaze enslaved me. Eric whispered against my trembling lips. "Do you trust me?"

"Yes," I breathed, fluttering my eyes. God, I didn't think I could ever say no to this man.

"Good girl." He broke our stare, nodding at Travis. A flash of black silk was the last thing I saw before it covered my eyes. I felt a firm tug from behind as he secured the blindfold in place.

"What are you doing?"

Eric placed his finger over my lips. "You're about to find out."

In one swift motion, I was swept off my feet. I could tell by the feel of the jersey against my skin that Eric was carrying me. Cool air hit my face as we walked out of the shower room. I turned my head toward the sound of the metal door opening. Where was he taking me? When the smell of freshly cut grass invaded my nose, I flew into a panic.

He's taking me out on the field? Has he lost his mind? We're going to get caught.

"Are you crazy? Someone will see us!" I shrieked, slapping my hand against his chest.

Eric eased me to my feet. He brushed his hands down my arms

as he spoke. "Relax, baby. No one's going to see us."

His words did little to calm me. "How can you be sure? What about campus security?"

"They don't patrol this end of campus again until three a.m. Everything is fine, I promise. Just trust me."

I did trust him. Completely. I knew he wouldn't risk something like this without taking every precaution, especially knowing how much was at stake for each of us.

When Eric sealed his mouth to mine, I immediately opened, eager to intensify the kiss. Each swipe of his tongue seemed to erase more of the fear from my body. I didn't notice that I was walking backward until I felt cold steel against my back. Instantly, I knew it was the goalpost. He was trying to replicate my fantasy...

Grabbing the sides of my face, he deepened our kiss and pressed me harder against the pole. I was so lost in our connection that I didn't realize my arms were being lifted above my head. Before I could protest, I heard the grinding sound of the handcuffs as they locked into place. I stepped forward, feeling the tension on my arms as I tugged against the post.

Relying on my senses, I swallowed hard, both terrified and exhilarated by what was happening around me.

"Relax, baby. We're going to make this a night you will never forget." Travis breathed as he pressed his mouth against the nape of my neck, trailing delicate kisses across my shoulder.

Suddenly, a hand brushed across my chest. "Your tits are so fucking perfect," Eric rasped from my opposite side before engulfing my breast into his mouth. I threw my head back and groaned as he flicked his tongue against my nipple.

Before I could recover, I felt a hand on the inside of my thigh.

"Open your legs up for me, Clare. Let me see how wet you are for us." Travis added pressure against my thigh, urging me to spread my stance. I obeyed his command and shivered when his hand continued its journey toward my pussy.

"Goddamn," he growled as his fingertips brushed across my drenched opening. "She's already soaked. That greedy little cunt wants our cocks, doesn't it?"

My answer came out in a cry when Eric's teeth sank into the flesh of my nipple. I tried to catch my breath, but Travis caught me off guard by plunging his fingers into my pussy, feverishly pumping his hand in and out of me. The delicious combination of pain and pleasure was enough to trigger the beginning of an orgasm.

"Oh, God," I screamed. I was just about to come when both Travis and Eric released me, leaving me primed and miserable. The ache in my core was so heavy that I began rocking my hips back and forth, desperately seeking some sort of relief.

"Not yet, baby. I want you to come on my cock," Travis panted against my ear.

The sound of the condom wrapper opening was heaven. Shaking with need, I began to whimper. "Please," I begged, my voice trembling. I didn't care who fucked me. I just needed someone inside me...now.

A hand trickled down my spine, sending shivers through my body. "Shhh. Be patient. Travis is going to make you feel so good, baby."

In my next breath, I was being hoisted up with two sets of hands. I felt my legs being positioned around Travis's waist as my arms were pulled behind my body, within the range of motion allowed by the cuffs.

"Give it to her. Make her fucking scream," Eric commanded.

With a low moan, Travis slowly pushed his length into me. My mouth fell open as his massive girth stretched my inner flesh.

"So fucking tight. Just like I remember," Travis gritted out.

Each powerful thrust yanked my arms against the restraints.

"That's it. Fuck that sweet, wet pussy. Make my girl come," Eric coached from behind me.

Biting through the pain in my wrists, I begged for him to give me more. "Harder, Travis. Fuck me harder."

Travis let out a loud curse, slamming into me with such force that it stole my breath. "That's right, baby. You've missed this cock, haven't you?"

"Yes, God, yes!"

The sharp sensation of his fingernails digging into my flesh triggered the delicious build in my core to intensify. My orgasm was right within reach, yet something seemed to be holding me back.

Eric's hand was fisting my hair, anchoring my head back against the goalpost. "Give it to him, Clare. Fucking come hard on his cock," he ordered, keeping his grip tight.

Eric's domineering tone was all it took to send me spiraling out of control. Clenching my inner walls, I shook in Travis's arms and cried my orgasm across the field. Travis held me still until I had come down from the climax.

"Jesus Christ, I almost came," he breathed, easing himself out of me. Travis gently lowered my body down until I felt the ground beneath my bare feet. He held me steady while Eric worked to free me from the cuffs. One by one, my aching arms dropped to my side.

Travis rubbed my sore arms. "I've got you."

I heard Travis's voice in front of me and felt Eric's warmth behind me, his hard cock pressing into my bottom. Smiling, I ground my ass against his hardness, begging for him to take me next.

The sound of approaching footsteps made me jump. Terrified that we'd just been caught, I buried my head into Travis's chest. "Who's there? What's going on?"

"It's okay, Clare. I promise." Travis kissed my forehead. "Take the blindfold off. It's time to let her see."

With a small tug, the silk fell from my eyes. I blinked hard, struggling to clear my vision. When I finally regained my focus, a shirtless football player stood before me. A pair of gray exercise shorts hung loosely from his lean hips. The black helmet on his head concealed his identity—a detail I found both erotic and terrifying. The mystery guy took a step forward, causing me to tremble.

"Breathe, baby," Eric whispered behind me.

"Who is he?" My voice shook.

"He's a friend, Clare. That's all you need to know."

Friend or not, I didn't want him out here watching us. Besides, what if he told someone?

I shot a look over at Eric. "I don't care. Tell him to leave."

"He's not going to leave, Clare. I asked him to come here."

My brows furrowed with confusion. "What? Why would you do that?"

He placed his hands on my shoulders. "Because I wanted to bring your fantasy to life."

"But I thought that was what we were doing before."

Smiling, he cupped my face in his hands. "No, baby, that was just the warm-up round. Get ready. We're about to make your wildest dreams come true."

ERIC

I shut everything inside me off, like I'd flipped a switch. It was better that way. If I allowed myself to get emotionally involved in this, I would lose my mind. I had to do this for Clare...for us.

"On your knees." Pressing down on Clare's shoulders, I urged her to the ground, and then tugged the football jersey over my head. I pulled my shorts down, took my cock in my hand, and stroked up and down the length. "Open that pretty little mouth up for me, baby."

I pumped my dick harder in my hand. Clare opened her mouth and stared up at me with those fucking incredible eyes, her gaze full of lust and need. I bit down on my bottom lip and watched as my cock disappeared between her lips. Greedy for more, I grabbed the back of her head, urging her to take all of me. I let out a loud groan when I felt the tip of my dick hit the back of her throat.

I cursed as she sealed her lips, creating a vacuum around my cock. Hot and moist, her mouth was like perfect sin. I bit the inside of my cheek, trying to keep control.

Tyler had his cock in his hand, no doubt eager for a taste of my girl. I gave him a nod, signaling him to join us. Once he was in front of her, I gave the command.

"Stroke him, Clare."

With her mouth still wrapped firmly around my dick, Clare reached over and took Tyler's shaft into her hand and pumped up and down. Tyler let out a loud, appreciative moan beside me. Still biting the inside of my mouth, I became entranced at the way her hand was moving over his cock. I could feel my climax building, but I had to fight it. I wasn't ready to come. Not yet. Not until I had sunk deep into her pussy.

When Travis stepped beside me, Clare wrapped one hand around his length, working both dicks with her fists in perfect sync.

"Suck them, Clare. Show them how incredible that mouth feels."

There was a loud pop as she released me from her mouth and moved toward Tyler. When he slid between Clare's plump lips, a pang of jealousy hit me hard. I fought against it, refusing to allow it to overtake me. I had to maintain control. No matter how much it fucking hurt to watch.

Clare switched to take Travis into her mouth, continuing to stroke up and down Tyler's length. I dropped to my knees behind her and delivered a hard blow against her ass cheek, eliciting a muffled moan around Travis's cock. When I repeated the action, she released him from her mouth, allowing me to urge her forward until she was on all fours. The beautiful view of her behind had me hard as fuck. I had to remind myself to not be greedy, to not take what I so desperately wanted to claim as mine.

As I spread her cheeks apart, her beautiful pink rim puckered out in anticipation. I wet my thumb, teasing the outside of the muscle before slowly sinking my finger into her. Clare let out a loud moan that shook through her body. My dirty girl loved anal play.

I added pressure, rotating my finger. Her greedy ass tugged hard against me, causing my cock to twitch. I retrieved my thumb from her opening and cursed at the way the muscles around her rim tightened back into place. It was as if they were taunting me for more. Right now, I would love nothing more than to fuck that ass. But I couldn't be selfish. Not tonight, at least.

I moved my hand forward, smiling at how drenched her pussy was. I eyed Tyler. "She's ready for you."

Nodding, he reached for one of the condoms on the ground, quickly ripping open the package.

"Go ahead, take her," I ordered, moving to the side to allow Tyler to kneel and position himself behind her.

He settled a trembling hand on her hip, using his other to align himself to her opening. I couldn't help finding amusement in his nervousness. No doubt about it, losing his virginity to Clare Winston would be something he'd never forget.

Tyler let out a loud curse from beneath the helmet as he sank into her pussy, stilling once he had fully seated her. Part of me envied him in that moment. I remembered the first time I'd been inside her. There was nothing in this world that could ever top that feeling.

Clare pushed against him, moaning.

"Move, she needs you to move."

Tyler pushed forward, picking up his pace with each thrust into her. Clare's eyes rolled back as the orgasm overtook her. Releasing Travis from her mouth, her eyes lifted to meet mine just as she screamed out her release.

"Holy fuck," Tyler shouted, pulling out of her. He knew the rules. Condom or not, no one was coming inside that pussy except me. And right now, I was aching to be balls deep inside her.

Dropping to my knees, I grabbed Clare by the waist and turned her until she was straddling me. Pellets of sweat glistened across her skin. Her beautiful face was flushed, her body still trembling from the multiple orgasms. I wouldn't be giving her time to recover. I was about to make her forget her fucking name.

I held her hips and shoved my cock up past the tight, wet lips of her cunt until I was completely consumed by her body. The strangled cry that escaped her lips woke the savage inside me. Holding nothing back, I fucked her, hard and unapologetically, until she was screaming out for more.

"Yeah? Do you like that, baby? Do you like how my thick cock feels inside you?"

Clare struggled to gain enough air to answer me. "Y-Yes!"

I sank my fingernails into her flesh, urging her to move faster against me. "Then, give it to me. Come on my fucking dick."

"Eric!" she screamed. When the warmth of her release drenched my shaft, I knew it was time. As I turned my head to the side, Travis and Tyler were fisting their cocks beside us.

"Now, Travis," I ordered, pulling Clare down against my chest, so her ass was high and open for him.

Travis had already rolled a new condom down his length. He moved behind her, grabbed the base of his cock, and, coating himself with her thick arousal, positioned himself at her rim.

I studied Clare's face as he entered her body, making certain that we weren't hurting her. All I could see was love and trust on her features.

She gasped, tensing in my arms. Once he was fully inside her, he froze in position, allowing her time to adjust to the fullness.

"Are you okay, baby?"

"God, yes." She panted. "More...I want more."

I held her against me, allowing Travis to control our movements. From this angle, I could feel the pressure of his cock pressing against the wall of muscle in her core. The sensation was so intense that it was everything I could do not to fucking explode inside her, right then and there. Tyler stepped closer, feverishly fisting his cock as he watched us fuck her. As if by instinct, Clare turned her head toward him, opening her mouth to receive him. His cock disappeared between her lips as he threw his head back and grunted as he released into her.

It was all I could do to hold on. Travis changed up things by rotating his hips. The slow shift was enough to cause Clare's inner walls to tense against us.

"Yes, oh, God. Just like that. Don't stop. Fuck...fuck...fuck!"

Clare screamed out her climax, triggering Travis and me to follow with our own.

I shouted out her name and held her hard against me as I came.

When Travis recovered, he placed a tender kiss on the middle of her back and eased out of her.

I tightened my embrace, savoring the fleeting contractions of her inner walls against my cock, aftershocks from our earth-shattering orgasm. Each gentle tug of her core made my balls ache for more. Gritting my teeth, I fought the urge to come again as I waited for Tyler and Travis to leave the field.

As they staggered away, leaving us alone, I rolled her to her back. Spreading her thighs apart, I took a moment to stare at her perfect pink opening.

She didn't know it yet, but this wasn't over.

◆ ◆ ◆ ◆

Bringing us both beneath the spray of the water, I placed a trail of delicate kisses across her shoulder and pushed my erection against her ass. Even after an intense follow-up round in the shower, I was ready to go again. I was desperate to stay in the moment with her. Desperate to string all of the seconds together. I was terrified if I let her go, this would be the end. Had this proven enough to her tonight? Had I erased enough of the doubts in her head?

Clare turned around, her eyes heavy with satisfaction. God, she was breathtaking. How could I ever have doubted that she would be enough for me?

She wrapped her arms around my neck before placing a tender kiss on my lips. "You're insatiable, you know that?"

"That's your fault. You're addictive."

"If we go another round, you're going to be carrying me around campus for the rest of the week. I can barely stand as it is."

"Mmm. I don't have a problem with that," I teased, walking her backward until her back was against the tile.

Clare giggled when I nuzzled into her neck, biting down on that sensitive spot right below her jaw.

She playfully slapped my chest. "Go get me a towel. I'm turning into a prune."

"Oh, really?" I grabbed her by the waist, spun her around, and delivered a hard slap across her bottom. "Nope, that ass still looks pretty perfect to me."

"Oh, my God, you're impossible." She laughed, using her hip to shove me out of the shower. "Now, go!"

I held my hands up. "Okay, okay. I'm going. No need to resort to violence," I teased.

As I wrapped my towel around my waist, my eyes caught the outline of my handprint that still lingered on her backside. The bright pink color that adorned her skin made my cock twitch. It took every bit of self-control I had not to take her up against that shower wall again. Jesus, would I ever get enough of this woman? Swallowing hard, I made my way to the locker room to grab an extra towel from my bag.

The sight of her clothes lying on the bench made me smile. My little seductress. In such a short amount of time, Clare's shyness had morphed into a sexy confidence—one of the only positive things that had resulted from our arrangement. I only hoped she felt the same way when she looked back on all of this.

I had just unzipped my bag when the screen on Clare's phone lit up, illuminating the dim locker room. I didn't want to violate her privacy, but my insecurity and curiosity trumped every rational thought that resided in me. Unable to restrain myself from looking, I picked up the phone. My heart plummeted as I read the message displayed on the screen. It was from Reed.

Megan told me everything. We need to talk. You need to know how I feel about you.

Anger.

Hurt.

Fear.

Every emotion seemed to come at me at once. As I stood there shaking, I knew I held the fate of our future in my hands. The line between right and wrong was obvious, but that didn't stop me from crossing it. Before I could talk myself out of it, I had already sent the reply from her phone.

It's too late. I've already made my decision. Don't contact me again.

I deleted the texts and returned her phone to where I'd found it. The guilt of my actions was heavy, yet bearable...especially if it meant protecting what was mine.

One harmless lie couldn't hurt us.

CHAPTER ELEVEN

CLARE

I sat on the bleachers, balancing my Psych notes and the corresponding textbook on my knees while I stole glances at Eric during his practice. He was glowing, rotating between grinning from camaraderie with his teammates and maintaining laser focus on the plays he'd need to execute with perfection for the next game. I fidgeted on the uncomfortable metal under my ass, because watching him sweat and command the field made me hotter than possibly anything or anyone else ever had. Not to mention that one glance at the goalpost filled me with some intensely hot memories.

I couldn't wait to steal a few minutes together in his room after practice. I was studying hard for the upcoming finals, but we'd resolved to spend as much time together as we could until the holiday break took us back to Ridgeville. I closed my eyes and remembered our extremely illegal encounter last week with Travis and another teammate who I'd yet to recognize. Unless he whipped his cock out on the field, I might never know the third party who'd given me pleasure that night. I was pretty sure we'd broken several college rules and a few county laws too. If that was the wildest encounter I had outside of my relationship with Eric, I could be happy with that.

Eric pushing for an open relationship had resulted in so many fulfilled sexual fantasies, most of which I had been too inexperienced to know I wanted before. While the pleasure had been tinged with a fair share of heartache, my eyes had been opened. I could say without a doubt that I knew my heart and my body better than I ever had. With this knowledge, I was ready to give one hundred percent to Eric and our exclusive relationship.

With two weeks left on the clock, I was certain the days would fly by because Eric was the only one I could see. And he didn't seem to mind one bit.

Practice wrapped and I packed my homework into my backpack before heading down to the field to see Eric. As he approached, Travis flanked him on the right.

Travis winked. "How were we out there tonight?"

I could feel myself blushing under his knowing stare. "Incredible. You guys make a great team."

He and Eric both chuckled.

"What are you up to tonight, Clare?"

Eric's humor disappeared and he shoved Travis off. "Get the fuck out of here."

Travis chuckled again and made his way toward the locker room while Eric moved close to me. He wasted no time in capturing my face and kissing me breathless.

"Sorry," he muttered after a few minutes. "I'm kind of gross right now."

I licked his lower lip before sucking it between my teeth. I released him with a hum, savoring his manly aroma. "I like the way you smell. It's like something inside me clicks and knows you're all I want."

He groaned and lowered one hand to my ass, pulling me close against his warm, strong body. He kissed me deeper, and I let the fantasies swirl through my mind.

"In fact..." I breathed between his intense kisses. "I wouldn't mind dropping down to my knees and blowing you right after your next big win. I want to taste the salt on your skin, all that sweat and effort lingering on your body before you get presentable again."

"Fuck me," he breathed, his cock growing hard against my belly. "You've become quite the dirty talker, haven't you, sweet Clare?"

I smiled against his lips. "Maybe I'm not so sweet anymore."

He squeezed my ass possessively. "Fine with me. Makes me love you even more. I like that you can tell me what you want, baby. Because I'm going to spend the rest of my life giving you exactly that."

My heart twisted, but the chatter of female voices reminded me that Eric and I weren't alone. A group of cheerleaders had arrived on the field for their own practice. Several of them were shooting surprised stares and a few glares our way. I wasn't stupid. I knew Eric was in high demand. Any one of those girls would drop to her knees for him on command. Didn't matter, though, because in two weeks that window of opportunity would close. As far as I was concerned, it was already closed.

"I know what I want right now, Eric."

He brushed my hair back and kissed my neck. "Tell me."

"Head back to the locker room, making no effort to disguise my effect on you so those girls know you're mine. And then I'll meet you at your place when you're done to thank you properly."

"Inching toward going public, are we?"

I shrugged. "I have nothing to hide."

"Neither do I. I'd streak the field if it meant watching my cock disappear between those pretty pink lips tonight."

I moaned and lifted on my toes, teasing my body along his as I moved. "If you got naked right now, those girls would claw each other's eyes out to get to you."

He laughed. "They've got nothing on you."

I breathed him in deeply once more before pushing back. "Hurry. I wish we had all night, but I need to finish studying for my Psych final after."

He bit his lip and brought his hand to the now-raging hard-on that poked against his practice shorts. God, what I'd give to pull them down and take him in my mouth right now. Right in front of all those bitches.

With a wink and a sly grin, he turned. He gave his erection a casual stroke while the girls watched him saunter past them and out of sight into the locker room. A few jaws dropped, a few more glares came my way. I answered them with a confident smile as I slung my bag over my shoulder and walked off the field.

They've got nothing on you.

For the first time in a long time, I truly believed Eric's words. He'd put me on a pedestal before, but I knew now, without a doubt, I could give Eric pleasure the way few others had. And he wasn't alone in that thought.

I was halfway to Eric's frat house when my phone dinged. It was Reed. My heart started to beat a little faster as I pulled up the text.

If that's what you really want, I won't contact you again. If you change your mind, I'll be here. I shouldn't have let so much time go by without talking to you about how I felt. My fault. I just want to know that you're happy, Clare.

My heart was racing now. I hadn't heard from Reed since I got back from Hawaii. We'd shared a couple friendly texts, but I'd been totally focused on Eric again so our communications died out quickly upon my return. Is that why he thought I didn't want him to contact me? I was so confused. I tapped out a reply.

What do you mean? I haven't heard from you since after the trip. I'm glad you reached out.

I hit send and then hesitated over the keyboard, knowing that what I really wanted to say shouldn't be said. Then again, he was four thousand miles away, and we'd likely never see each other again. What harm could it do to let him know a little bit of how I felt?

I miss you.

I sent the second message, intending to stuff my phone away and continue on my journey when Reed's quick reply came back.

I texted you last week after I talked to Megan. I've missed you too. You said you didn't want me to contact you again. If you're with him now, I understand.

Frowning, I scrolled up through our previous messages, but all I could see were the texts we'd shared after I'd gotten home from Hawaii. Nothing from last week. Dread and embarrassment slid through my veins.

I'm sorry. That wasn't me.

I stood frozen in place. I could ignore this. I could shut my phone off and go meet Eric, have an hour or so of incredible sex, and then return to my studies. But I was certain that someone had tampered with my phone, and I was pretty sure it had been Eric. Who else would have the motivation to lie to Reed? What if Reed hadn't reached out to me again...ever? Fresh anger washed over me as I pivoted and made strides toward my dorm. As I did, I called Reed.

The phone rang only once before he picked up, his deep, luscious voice greeting me on the other end.

"Clare."

"Reed. I'm so sorry. I don't know what happened, but I didn't send that text."

He exhaled audibly. "You have no idea how relieved I am to hear that. I thought I'd made a mistake reaching out to you. I don't want to upset you, but Megan made it sound like you were dealing with a lot right now and might want to talk."

I shook my head, silently cursing Megan for getting involved in my shit. That's the thanks I got for giving her the full scoop, but I also knew deep down that she had my best interests in mind. She only wanted me to be happy.

"She wasn't wrong. It's been an intense few months." I was silent a beat before continuing. "I've thought a lot about our time together, Reed. It was really special. I don't know if we'll ever cross paths again, but—"

"Clare, I bought tickets to come out there this weekend."

"What?"

"Cole is going out to see Megan. They had a fun time, and I figured I could tag along and if you wanted to see me, we could talk. But ever since you sent that text, I wondered if I'd made the wrong call. I still want to see you, Clare."

Shit. The last thing I needed was a beautiful blond surfer hanging around my dorm room while Paul and Eric devised ways to kill him. Before I could search for an excuse to turn him down, he continued.

"I don't want to cause any drama in your life. Cole booked a room near Megan's university. I could come and hang out there. But I don't want to put any pressure on you."

God, he was being so perfect. I wanted to slap the shit out of Eric for being so deceitful. I should have let my anger settle. I should have talked to Eric and set the record straight, but a little voice in my head reminded me that we had two weeks left on this agreement, and under those terms, if I went to see Reed, I wasn't breaking any rules.

"I want you to come, Reed," I said, and the truth of the words warmed my chest. "I miss you. I'd love to see you again."

ERIC

My cock was aching by the time I got to the frat house and scaled the stairs up to my room. The door was locked, and when I unlocked it, I found the room empty. Confused, I shot a concerned text to Clare. She'd had plenty of time to get here before me.

Where are you?

I paced around, waiting for her reply. Another minute I was going to retrace her steps from the field and check her dorm to make sure she was okay. The late fall nights were getting dark earlier. I shouldn't have let her walk home on her own. Then she replied.

I had to head back to my place. Professor dropped a last-minute assignment on us for next week. I'm sorry.

"Damnit," I muttered.

She'd gotten me all worked up with those promises of her mouth, and she bailed? Oh well, I couldn't get in the way of her academics. I knew she loved me, but I also knew she had to work hard to keep her scholarship.

I couldn't wait for school to be over, and I couldn't wait for the lease to run out on this agreement. I wasn't really worried about her hooking up with other people since we were around each other nonstop lately, but I couldn't shake an uneasy feeling that her exclusivity wasn't guaranteed yet. Fucking was fucking, but Paul had gotten close to her heart. And whatever she'd confided in her friend Megan had inspired this Reed guy to reemerge. Hopefully I'd closed that down, even if the guilt still nagged at me a bit. My selfish need to have her all to myself made me feel justified, even if I'd betrayed her trust by shutting him down.

I dropped down onto the bed and stared at the pile of books I should have been peeling through. But my muscles were tired and I couldn't keep my thoughts away from Clare. This arrangement had taken a toll on me this first term, but by some miracle I'd been able to keep my grades sufficiently above the line to qualify me to keep playing.

When I was playing, it was easy to forget about Clare and immerse myself in the game. Homework was another story. She was everywhere—memories of her body, the sound of her sweet voice in my head. If I knew she was mine, really truly mine, committed to only me, maybe I could find a little bit of peace and actually get something out of college. Football was my dream, but those kinds of dreams didn't last forever. I needed to fall back on something when my arm gave out one of these days.

Still, I couldn't bring myself to shift into study mode. I grabbed my phone. Seeing no more texts from Clare, I dialed my parents' home number. My mom picked up, her kind voice saying my name like I was still a toddler running into the room to his momma.

"Mom, I wanted to talk to you about Christmas break."

"What is it? Don't tell me you're taking some trip with your friends. We were looking forward to spending some time you with, especially since you took off after Thanksgiving."

I sighed. "I'm sorry about that, Mom. I want to stay at home and catch up with you guys. But I want to bring someone."

"The girl?" She couldn't hide the intrigue in her voice.

"Yeah. Clare's dad isn't really...supportive, I guess. She could stay there, but I'd rather have her stay with us and have real family time."

"She's important to you," she said, her tone kind.

"Yeah."

She had no idea.

"Of course, she can stay, Eric. I'm just so..." I heard her swallow and suck in a tiny breath on the other end of the phone. "I'm so happy you found a girl. I never really warmed to Mandy. I never wanted to say anything, because you were having so much fun. I just want you to find someone who deserves you. Someone worth really investing in for the long-term."

"That's Clare. She's the only one I want, and I can't see that ever changing right now. I can't wait for you to meet her."

"I can't wait to meet her either. Don't you worry about a thing, sweetheart. We'll make this holiday special for her."

"Thanks, Mom. I'll talk to you soon."

I hung up, grateful that I'd always had such a supportive family. Clare had always been so sheltered, so shell-shocked from her broken family. Was pushing her out into the world the way I had been a good idea? God knows it hadn't always been easy to stomach, but I hoped if we ended up together, forever, that she could look back and know that she'd experienced enough before I stole her away from everyone else.

I fell back on the bed with a sigh. When I closed my eyes, thoughts of my beautiful girl flooded my mind. Every look, every little moan, knowing I'd been the first one to push past her virginity and deep into that warm little pussy. *Fuck*... I unfastened my jeans, fisted my cock, and stroked it with Clare's name on my lips.

CLARE

Friday night came, and I stared out the window as the bus took me toward Megan's campus. My dorm would be a ghost town tonight because of the home game. No one would miss me, except Eric. I hadn't missed a game all season, but I was still pissed and unsettled about what he'd done.

I didn't bother telling him I'd be spending the weekend with Megan until he texted me before the game. He hadn't bothered telling me that Reed had reached out, and I decided he deserved a dose of his own medicine. When he didn't reply, I figured he was mad, and likely put together that I might be seeing Reed.

I didn't regret upsetting him. Even when I thought this last infidelity might break us apart forever, I recognized a measure of strength in myself that hadn't existed before. I loved Eric, but if we were to have a future, he couldn't betray my trust like this again. Never again. I'd come too far and endured too much to let him puppeteer my life the way he had most of my sexual experiences.

The bus stopped downtown, and after a quick exchange with Megan, I headed down the main street to the Indian restaurant where she, Cole, and Reed were getting dinner. My stomach fluttered with nerves, the good and bad kind. Nothing was simple about seeing Reed again after so long. Every move I made felt dangerous. I had no idea how he'd make me feel after all this time.

As I entered the restaurant, the aroma of curries and garlic filled my nostrils. My stomach groaned, because I had been too nervous to eat all day. In a second, I spotted them at a table in the corner. Reed stood immediately, taking easy strides toward me. My breath caught. He was a Hawaiian beach god, transported as if by magic to this little college town. Tall, tanned, and ripped with lean muscle, he wore a striped blue and white collared shirt that hung past his waist over his jeans. His eyes were dark as he approached, hungry and warm and everything I'd remembered.

In an instant, I was back on the island with him. Tangled in his sheets, coming over and over again as his gaze riveted with mine, like we were one—two people overwhelmed with the same incredible sensations. Had sex ever been like that?

When he reached for me, I didn't hesitate. I threw my arms around him and let him hold me hard against him, like we were two long-lost lovers. We were...

"Clare," he whispered against my ear, his strong arms keeping me firmly against him. "Goddamn, I missed you so much."

I nuzzled against his neck, and I swore to God he smelled like the ocean. Like sunshine and the waves that he could glide over like magic. "I missed you too."

I wasn't sure how many minutes went by before we separated, but eventually we had enough sense to go back to Megan and Cole. Cole rose and gave me a hug, only after shooting a knowing grin to Reed.

We spent the next hour catching up on life since our last meeting. Megan and I talked about college life. Cole was wrapping up his studies in Hawaii too, and Reed was still making a name for himself as a professional surfer, an occupation that had taken him around the world and earned him valuable sponsorships.

I warmed with pride, as affected as I'd been before when I was this close to him. Reed Michaels had charisma. His charm, good looks, and easy nature radiated like rays off the tropical sun. I'd been drawn to him from the day he'd tossed his Frisbee my way on the beach. It was no wonder he'd taken up residence in my thoughts since then. He was a dream.

I was lost in my thoughts when Cole picked up the check, and Reed caught my hand under the table. Again, his heat seemed to envelop me, seeping under my skin, burning me down to my core, where simply being in his presence made me pulse with desire. We headed out and paused outside the restaurant.

"Well, I guess Reed and I should head back to the hotel." Cole slapped his hands together and then rubbed them together, shooting a tentative look between Reed and Megan.

Megan smirked. "It's still early, Cole. I could show you around campus."

Cole nodded, and Reed glanced over at me. "Megan's right. The night is young. Want to hang out downtown with me a bit?"

If the invitation wasn't so heavy with expectation, I may have laughed out loud at our very friendly and covert negotiations of sleeping arrangements. Without a doubt, I wanted more of Reed's time. But if I ended up in his room, I'd end up in his bed too. I was angry with Eric, but I wasn't completely sure I wanted to cross that line with Reed again.

I shot Megan a look that I hoped was more confident than I felt. "Sure, that sounds like a good plan. I guess we'll see you guys later."

After a brief goodbye, Megan and Cole were headed down the street toward campus, already hand in hand. Whatever went down with Reed tonight, I was confident my best friend would enjoy a reunion with her own Hawaiian hookup.

I startled slightly when Reed slid his warm hand into mine again and tugged me gently toward him. "Come on. Let's get you some ice cream."

I smiled, happy once again to be with him, and flooded with relief that we weren't headed right to bed.

ERIC

I was sore and miserable. I'd played like shit. We won by a single point in the fourth quarter, thanks to the Hail Mary I'd thrown and Travis's ability to find it and take it into the end zone. My teammates were supportive, but their reassurances were weak, and I could see the disappointment in their eyes. Then Coach removed all doubt by tearing me a new one. He was right. My head wasn't in the game. I'd been somewhere else the whole goddamn night.

I'd texted Clare before the game, hoping we could meet up after and she could make good on the little fantasy she'd painted earlier in the week. But she was spending the weekend with Megan and seeing some friends. I didn't have to ask why. I nearly broke my phone, but thought better of it, since it would be my only lifeline to her while she was gone.

She'd blown off the game, and me...for someone who I thought I'd effectively banned from her life forever. The violent jealousy hadn't done me any favors on the field, though. I was too emotional to play well and make smart decisions.

Chances were high that she'd have her last hurrah with Reed, but what had she told Megan? Did he have a piece of her heart that she just couldn't deny? Did she love him?

I barreled my fist into a nearby locker when I thought about that possibility. I was a fucking loser. Too stupid to keep the best thing that had ever happened to me.

"Hey, is everything okay?" A pretty brunette dressed in her cheer uniform peeked around the door of the empty locker room.

I shook my head, ignoring her. "I'm fine. Go away."

But she didn't leave. She came closer, not saying a word. Before I could say anything more, she was on her knees, unfastening my belt and rubbing me suggestively through my jeans.

"What are you doing?"

She gazed up at me through her thick brown lashes and brought a finger to her lips. "Shhh."

I was still tense, but she kept moving, unzipping my pants and pulling my semi-hard cock out of my boxer briefs. I closed my eyes. I was so fucking wound up. So fucking angry and hurt. Why the hell couldn't she be Clare right now? I needed her. I needed her warmth, her touch, her lips...

"Ahhh," I gasped when the girl's lips came around my cock. She'd taken me down to the back of her throat immediately, probably trying to impress me enough to date her after I blew my load.

"I'm not looking for a girlfriend, you know."

She pulled off my cock for a second and stared up at me. "I don't really give a shit, Eric. You had a rough game, and I just want to suck you off. I'm not asking for anything else."

I nodded. She made a compelling argument under the current circumstances. "Then put my cock back in your mouth, sweetheart."

She smirked and went to work, slickening my cock with her spit and swirling her tongue around my length as far as she could go once I was fully hard. I was aroused, but it wasn't enough. This girl was pretty, but she just wasn't doing it for me. At this rate, her jaw would give out before I would come.

"Let me see your tits."

Without a moment's hesitation or unlatching her mouth, she lifted her V-neck sweater up and pushed her bra down her waist, revealing her naked chest. Her tits were big, double Ds for sure. She pinched her big, light brown nipples until they hardened. Nice set, but they weren't Clare's perky pair, with nipples poking out like little strawberries ripe to be picked. With my mouth and teeth.

I let my head fall back against the locker, giving up on the visuals this girl was giving me. I just focused on the feeling, matching up her decent oral skills with the vision of my beautiful Clare. The arousal that had prickled and gotten me to this point began to grow, tightening my balls and sending the orgasm rushing down my spine. I was going to come. In my mind, Clare opened her mouth the way she had for Tyler last week. The girl's mouth sucked and stroked me, faster and firmer, and then I came hard...in Clare. In her mouth, my hot release coating her velvety tongue.

Eyes closed to stay with my half-fantasy, I groaned and shuddered, spilling everything I had into the willing mouth below. *Clare...Clare.* I wanted to say her name so badly.

I opened my eyes at the sound of the door opening. Travis came in, showered and dressed.

"Whoa, you okay?" His eyes went wide at the position I was in.

I nodded and put my cock back in my pants, where I probably should have kept it. I felt better, but I also felt a hell of a lot worse.

The brunette stayed on her knees. She gazed up at me and then to Travis.

"Rough night?" Her voice was a throaty purr that might have turned me on again if I hadn't been sated.

Lust darkened Travis's eyes. "Yeah, real rough."

The corner of her mouth lifted and she curled her finger, motioning him toward her. I stepped away, seeing where this was headed. I grabbed my bag of gear and headed for the door. I only glanced back once. Travis stood where I had against the lockers, dick in hand, guiding it into the girl's eager mouth with a groan.

She gave good head, but she wasn't Clare. Not in a million years.

CLARE

Reed held my hand in his while I rested my head against his shoulder. We sat on a bench overlooking a small park. The sunset had faded, and the night had grown dark and cool.

"Do you want to head back to the hotel for a while?"

I glanced up to Reed's beautifully bronzed face. Hesitating, I chewed the inside of my lip.

His brow wrinkled. "Clare...we don't have to do anything. I hope you know that's not why I came here."

I stared down to where our fingers wove together. "Megan told me that you had things you wanted to say to me."

He sighed and nodded. "Yeah. I guess I've been stalling because I don't know where you're at with this guy."

"Eric."

His expression tightened. "Right. Eric."

I exhaled and leaned against Reed's shoulder again as fatigue took a stronger hold on me. "It's complicated."

"You love him."

I nodded. "Very much."

"Then why can't you forget about us?"

I hesitated. I knew we'd have to address this eventually. Megan had evidently told him almost everything. "I guess because I've never been with someone like you. Someone who was so careful with me. When we were together, we had this connection that I haven't been able to forget."

He touched my cheek and tipped my face up. "Then let's try to make this work."

I winced and closed my eyes. "That's impossible."

"Why?"

"For starters, you live in Hawaii."

"I travel all over the world."

"Exactly, and this do-nothing town shouldn't be a regular pit stop for you."

"Then transfer to Hawaii."

I laughed. "I love that you dream, Reed. I'm sure that's why you're as successful as you are. But I can't afford to live on the island, let alone pay for school there. I have an amazing scholarship here that I couldn't leave even if I wanted to."

He sighed and stared up into the darkening sky. "I was afraid you'd say all that."

My shoulders hunched. "And you traveled four thousand miles to hear me say it. I'm sorry, Reed."

"I made the trip to see you and spend time with you. That's what we're doing. You don't owe me anything."

Emotion clogged my throat and stung my eyes. "Reed..."

He hushed me and pulled me in closer to him, wrapping his arms around me. As I cried into his chest, relief, sadness, love, and even a glimmer of hope washed over me.

When I caught my breath, I chanced a look up into Reed's dark, soulful eyes, hoping that somewhere in those depths he held the answers to the many questions swirling through my mind right now.

"Clare, you're special. I'm sorry you're going through all this, but I know that if you follow your heart, it'll take you where you need to be. And no matter what you decide, I'll be here—or somewhere—a phone call or a plane ride away. As a friend, a lover, a shoulder to cry on. You're one of the purest, kindest people I've ever met, and I want you in my life any way I can have you. We made love, and it was incredible. I'll never forget a second of it, but that's not why I'm here. I'm here for you. Okay?"

Fresh tears brimmed my eyes as I nodded. "Thank you, Reed." I sucked in a deep breath and tried to pull myself together. "God, I'm so tired. Do you want to head back now?"

"Sure. Let's go."

Ten minutes later I was on the top floor of the nicest hotel this little college town had to offer. The room had two queen-size beds and a view of the downtown.

Reed tossed his light jacket onto the couch. "I'm going to take a quick shower if you don't mind. I've been traveling all day, and I didn't get a chance to clean up much before."

"Of course. Take your time."

"Want to pick out a movie or something? We can just relax tonight, order room service or whatever."

My lips curved upward. "That sounds perfect."

He winked before disappearing into the bathroom. I unpacked and quickly changed into comfortable pajama pants and a light T-shirt for bed, still in slight disbelief that Reed had come all this way for a sexless slumber party with me. I felt like such a bitch, but I also felt honored and appreciated. Reed had had that effect on me before. He'd taken his time with me, really taken care of me while we were together. The mere remembrance made my desire surge. Good God, how was I going to get through this night?

ERIC

My head was swimming. The frat house punch was lethal, and I'd had no less than ten cups of it. I couldn't wait to pass out, because then I could escape the stares and thoughts that had been tormenting me all goddamn night. The wall was holding me up as I watched a game of beer pong play out. Travis was about to lose after a pretty lengthy winning streak.

He downed the last solo cup and came to me, slapping me on the arm. "What's with the long face, man? We won. You're still acting like we lost."

I let out a weak laugh. "Yeah, should have heard how happy Coach was about that win."

He shrugged. "Who cares? We'll kill it next week."

"You saved the game," I said.

"And you threw the winning pass. We're a team, like always."

I knew then I was past drunk, because I was ready to give the motherfucker a hug and thank him for being the best friend I'd ever had. If only he could save me from this awful mess I'd made with Clare.

"Have you ever been in love, Travis?"

He let out a long sigh and grabbed my arm. "Come on. I have a feeling we need some fresh air for this conversation."

I followed him upstairs and outside to where a stained floral couch sat on an upper deck.

"Okay, to answer your question, I'm not really sure. Sometimes I think I'm in love with Tori, but I've never fucked her so I'm not sure if I can commit to love without knowing how we'd be together physically."

My eyes went wide. "You think you're *in love* with her? Why the hell didn't you date her when we were still in school?"

He shrugged again, looking less confident than he had before. "I don't know. I wanted to mess around. I figured if I locked it down with her, it would only last through high school and then, like you and Mandy, we'd end up going our separate ways. If I was going to be with her, I wanted to just be with her and really make it last."

"And now?"

He shoved his hand through his hair and took another swig of beer. "I don't want to talk about me. Why'd you ask me that anyway? Is this about Clare?"

"I think she's fucking someone else right now."

He locked on me with a frozen stare. "Uh, do we need to go kill someone?"

"No. I gave her permission. A long time ago."

"Is this another fantasy thing like we did with Tyler?"

"No, at the beginning of the semester I told her that she should have experiences with other people, and so could I. And we agreed to do that until Christmas. One more week and then it'll just be us. No one else."

He shook his head. "I don't understand it, but whatever. If that's the deal though, why aren't you balls deep in cheer squad pussy right now?"

"Because she's the only one I want."

He rubbed his forehead with a sigh. "All right. One more week then. And in the meantime, put her out of your head because I can't deal with your fucking moping."

"But what if she changes her mind? What if she falls for this guy, and I lost my chance by trying to give her the freedom I thought she needed?"

He frowned and leaned toward me. "Then you fucking win her back. You don't pussy out on the field and you don't give up on the girl you love. You tell her how you feel and you prove it to her. That's it."

I clenched my jaw tight and nodded. Travis was right. I couldn't give up, and it wasn't fair of me to make her feel guilty for the arrangement I'd forced on her.

Travis stood abruptly. "I'm not drunk enough. You want a beer?"

I shook my head. "Nah, I'll hang out here for a bit."

As soon as he left, I fished my phone out of my pocket and dialed Clare's number. I didn't expect her to pick up. When her voicemail greeting played out, I closed my eyes at the sound of her sweet voice. Then a beep.

"Hey, Clare. It's me. I figure you're probably with this guy tonight." I swallowed hard. "That's okay. I just wanted you to know that I'm thinking about you. I missed you tonight. God, I wish you were here just so I could hold you. I know I don't deserve it right now. I fucked up. I've fucked up so much with us. All I can do is beg you to give me a chance to make it right. One more week...and then I want to start all over. Just you and me. That's all I ever want." I exhaled a shaky sigh and fought the emotion coming to the surface too quickly. "Sorry. Damnit, I'm too drunk for this. But I just wanted you to know how I felt. Let me know when you're back and maybe we can talk. I love you, Clare. Bye..."

CHAPTER TWELVE

CLARE

The weekend with Megan went almost nothing how I'd expected. In my mind, I imagined that I was running from Eric and his bad behavior and straight into Reed's arms. I had little doubt that we'd end up in his bed. We had, but I hadn't let him into my body. He didn't even kiss me until we'd said goodbye. Something told me I wasn't going to be seeing him again for a long time, so I let him kiss me senseless. He promised me again that he'd always be there for me, and the way he'd proven to me that he could be a friend without sex in the equation made me really believe him. Maybe there was a way to go backward from a hookup and find true friendship. And maybe *that* was what had brought him back into my life this second time, with a fate of friendship, not love.

As I sat on the bus that would take me back to my campus and my life, I pulled my phone out and absently went through the motions of checking my apps and my email. I went to my voice messages and thought about replaying Eric's drunken message from Friday night. I'd checked the score online. They'd barely won. I wasn't sure if I could have alleviated the guilt if they'd lost. The big game was this coming weekend, and then we'd both be heading home to Ridgeville.

When I arrived back at the dorm, Lacey was sitting at her desk with her nose in a book. She lifted her head and nodded toward my desk. "You got a delivery. I wasn't sure when you were getting back. Eric's been here a few times looking for you."

On my desk was a beautiful bouquet of fall flowers arranged in a short crystal vase. The aroma filled the room. And even though my first instinct was to call Eric, fly into his arms, and fuck until we couldn't be angry with each other anymore, I resisted the temptation.

Eric had his game and I had my own academic pressures. We had to talk, but we both had a lot riding on us this week. Beyond that, I had no idea what I would say right now. Everything was about to change. Things *had* to change...

"Lacey, if he comes by again, can you cover for me? Just let him know I'm at the library or something? I need this week to get through finals, and he's the ultimate distraction."

Lacey hesitated. "Sure, but he looks kind of desperate. Can you at least call him or something?"

I shook my head with a sigh. "It's complicated. I can't really see him right now."

She held my stare. "Are you breaking up with him?"

I laughed and dropped down onto my bed. "We'd have to be dating for me to break up with him."

"You know what I mean. You're together, like it or not."

I shrugged, ignoring her persistence. I knew she meant well, but I was done with everyone's advice. The only voice I could hear right now was Reed's, telling me to follow my heart. I had to choose my own path. No one could choose it for me.

ERIC

Under my advisor's tutelage, I'd signed up for every class I could breeze through to allow maximum time for sports. And that's exactly what I did during finals week. I knew Clare's classes were much more challenging, and I didn't envy her.

The week wasn't without its stresses, however. It'd been almost two weeks without seeing Clare, and I felt like I was starving. Cut off from everything that made life worth waking up for.

She'd texted me only once. A simple message thanking me for the flowers and saying that she'd come see me when her finals were through. But that wasn't nearly enough to take the edge off. I needed to touch her. I wanted to breathe her air. I had to make love to her, because it was the only way I knew how to break down every wall between us.

Right now, I was outside the wall she'd built around herself, and I had no idea how to push past it. Tonight I had to focus on the game. My future at this school depended on it. Once we got past this week, though, I'd be merciless.

The lights glowed above the field, and the crowd was roaring with anticipation. I felt the pressure to perform deep in my bones. Even though I was warmed up, my muscles jumped from the nerves. I was edgy and fully at war with myself. Doubts that I could pull this off clawed for attention in my brain.

I shook my head, trying to dislodge them, and threw a practice pass to Travis. I had to focus. I had to envision the win. And I had to get the fear of losing Clare out of my head.

Travis tossed the ball back, and I heard a girl's voice call out my name. I glanced over my shoulder to where the cheerleaders were lined up. The brunette from the locker room was shaking her pompoms, doing her job to get the crowd and the team pumped up. Her cheerful gaze was fixed on me, but just past her, in the bleachers, another face caught my eye.

Clare was there, dressed in our colors. Her strawberry-blond hair curled around her face and fell over her shoulders. I thought my heart was going to fucking explode. Suddenly, I had oxygen again when I'd been deprived of it for days. I had sustenance, Clare in the flesh, when I'd been surviving only on memories. My feet froze in the turf, but every cell in my body wanted to propel me to her. Because in that single moment, we were the only two people who existed. She was my Clare. The same sweet girl who'd cheered me on from the stands all through school whether I'd known it or not. The same brave girl who'd given herself to me so completely. By some miracle, with hundreds of people cluttering the view, then and now, she had come into focus.

I mouthed the words, "I love you," to her. Her eyes glittered with emotion.

My nerves calmed. Everything was clearer. Then Travis hollered my name, drawing my attention back to the field. I pulled back and arrowed the ball right into his hands.

The game sped by. The opposition came at us hard, but we were a force to be reckoned with. I saw every play before it happened. Split-second decisions moved us down the field with speed and accuracy. I'd never felt more a part of the team I'd spent the whole semester playing with.

We didn't just win. We destroyed them.

Coach came out onto the field with the other staff after the final whistle blew. He slapped me hard on the arm that wasn't sore from throwing passes. "Good job, son. I'll be a son of a bitch if they don't go running home crying to their mommas after that game."

I laughed and let him pull me in for a manly hug. Before the team could drag me into the locker room, I sprinted to the sideline where Clare stood among the cheering masses. I scaled the stands to the second row, pushed past a couple people who stood between us, and hauled her against me. She parted her lips to say something, but I stole her words with a kiss. The fierce claiming of her mouth was met with a fresh roar of hoots and cheers around us.

Relief flooded every vein. Relief that we'd won. That Clare was back in my arms. That the rest of the school knew she was mine. The greatest relief came with the promise that maybe our future wasn't lost.

I pulled away only to catch my breath. "See me tonight."

She smiled tearfully, her pink lips wet and swollen from my kisses. "No, you go celebrate with your team. They deserve it. You deserve it."

I frowned. "Clare..." Goddamn, this woman was going to kill me.

She shook her head and put a little pressure on my chest. "Go, they want to see their hero. We'll talk later."

Against every instinct, I pulled away. But not before I took her lips one last time. I stopped just before my cock started throbbing. It was one thing to let the cheerleaders know Clare Winston made me hard as a fucking rock. It was another to let the entire campus know it.

CLARE

I didn't sleep much the night of Eric's win. The adrenaline that had surged through me during the game had barely waned hours later, making me jumpy and energized when I should have been resting for the journey home tomorrow.

Lacey had left campus with her parents after the game, so I killed time tidying up our room and packing my bags for the trip home. The longing that Eric had inspired with his very public kiss only sharpened as the hours passed. Just past midnight I'd given up trying to get him out of my head. Falling into bed, I slid my hand into my panties and hurriedly brought myself to orgasm. I cried out, Eric's name on my lips, my pussy slick and ready for him. The relief was fleeting, and hell if the ache to have him filling me up with his cock wasn't sharp as ever afterward.

Early the next morning, fueled with only a few hours of sleep, I texted Paul, asking him to meet me for coffee. He agreed, and the prospect of seeing him filled me with a fresh wave of uneasiness. The semester was over, and I couldn't help but feel like I'd made an utter mess of my social life.

Even though I'd managed to avoid talking to Paul, I knew we needed to sit down and hash things out if I had any chance of saving our friendship. Unlike the level-headed Reed, Paul was hurt and overly emotional about the fact that I'd slept with him. I'd given him time to process everything and hopefully understand once and for all that we couldn't have a romantic future together.

Whether or not he had come to this realization on his own, I cared enough about keeping him in my life to make sure I gave him the right reasons to stay.

He was waiting at a table in the campus café when I arrived. I ordered a coffee and took the seat opposite his.

"Hi," I said, my voice barely above a whisper.

"Hey." He adjusted his glasses and kept his stare fixed on the tabletop between us.

"I'm sorry about everything, Paul."

He lifted his gaze, his eyebrow arched. "You're sorry?"

"I should have been more careful with our friendship. It makes me sick to think that I've jeopardized that."

He winced, and sadness washed across his features. "Clare, I'm still your friend. I just wish I could be more."

I nodded. "I know that now. I'm sorry if I misled you. I tried to be honest with you."

"You were. You told me everything. I just couldn't bring myself to believe it."

I sighed, hating that I'd hurt my friend so much. "I want you to know that this isn't about Eric. It's not about me choosing him over you or anything like that."

His lips tightened. "Sure feels that way."

I reached over and grabbed his hand, pulling it toward me. "I don't compare everyone in my life to him and then decide how I feel. I really care about you, Paul. You're my friend for reasons that have nothing to do with him and everything to do with the time we've shared together this year. We've gotten to know each other a lot. I respect you, and I love being around you. You make me laugh. You're the best study buddy a girl could have."

He met my small smile with one of his own.

"Promise me that we haven't lost that," I said, my voice a whisper.

He tightened his hold on my hand, threading our fingers together before leaning in and holding me with his warm green gaze. "Loving you doesn't mean I can't be your friend, Clare. It just means that I have to honor the boundaries you've set for our relationship. I respect that now. And if anyone should be sorry, it should be me. I came on strong, and I basically lied when I said that I could accept one night in your bed for what it was...one night. That was selfish of me."

I took comfort in the warmth of his hand in mine. The muscles that once held tension in anticipation of this conversation began to relax. "I forgive you, okay?"

His smile broadened. "Good."

"Friends?"

He nodded. His mouth softened and his gaze grew warm with affection. "Friends."

ERIC

"Where is Clare?" My mom didn't bother hugging me when I stepped through the door. Instead she stared at me with wide-eyed concern.

"Hello to you too, Mom," I muttered, though the same question had been on my mind over the four-hour drive back home. I'd partied with my pals all night, nursed a decent hangover the next morning, and by the time I got to Clare's dorm later that day, both Lacey and she were gone.

She'd never given me a chance to officially invite her to stay with me back in Ridgeville for the holiday. I didn't expect she'd say yes anyway. Things had been too shaky between us. Didn't change the fact that I wasn't going to go another day without her. I was done waiting.

"Did she dump you already?" My little brother piped up from his reclining posture on the couch where he was busy killing zombies on the latest video game.

My jaw tensed, and I fought the urge to rain hell on that little twerp. "No, she didn't dump me. I'm going to see her right now."

My mother nodded, but worry wrinkled her forehead. "And you'll bring her back?"

"I'm not leaving there without her. I should be back for dinner." I dropped my bags and turned for the door.

Fifteen minutes later, I was on the south side of town, a far cry from the manicured lawns and newly developed neighborhoods where my parents' home was. When the economy tanked, many of the homes in this part of town went vacant. I drove slowly, scanning home after home for Clare's house. I parked when I spotted the modest white ranch where Clare had grown up. The lawn was overgrown, and the vinyl siding was battered from years of weather.

I went to the front door and knocked. A steady murmur and the sound of voices filtered through the door, but no one answered. I knocked again, longer and louder, but still nothing. I was too amped, too goddamn determined to turn back now. I turned the knob and opened the door into a darkened living room. The television blared loudly with a college football game, and the light from the screen danced across the face of a man I guessed was Clare's father. He lay motionless on the couch, and his stale odor hit my nostrils around the same time I realized he was completely passed out. A nearly empty handle of vodka was the centerpiece on a coffee table otherwise littered with empty frozen dinner containers and trash.

Something slammed farther into the house, and I followed the sound into the kitchen. Clare was at the counter, earbuds tucked into her ears, her hands moving feverishly over the surface—putting things away, tossing others in the nearby trash, and wiping a clean path as she went.

My heart wanted to leap at the sight of her, but instead it felt like it was breaking, knowing this is how she'd lived before she left for college. Good God...

I came up behind her, placing a hand gently at her back. She twisted with a scream before slapping her hand over her mouth.

"Eric, you scared the shit out of me."

"Sorry."

Realization seemed to hit when her gaze darted around the messy kitchen and then back to me. "What are you doing here?"

"I had to see you. I promised my mom I was going to bring you home with me. You never gave me that chance."

Her face fell. I drew my fingertips down her cheek and brushed my lips over hers before she could say no.

"Eric." Her voice was a breathless whisper. "We need to talk."

"Take me to your room."

Her gaze fluttered up to mine, but she only hesitated a moment before taking my hand and leading me to the back of the house. Unlike the rest of what I'd seen, Clare's room was immaculate. Neat and organized and very much a girl's room. Light lavender paint, pictures on the walls, and a white lacy duvet covering her twin bed.

I moved slowly around the room, taking in the details. The area above her small writing desk was decorated with awards from her academic achievements at Ridgeville High.

"You did all this on your own." I glanced back at her, not because I needed her to agree, but because I wanted her to know I understood. One look at this place, and I could see plain as day that she'd had virtually no support. Least of all from the poor excuse of a human holding down the couch right now.

She nodded with a swallow. "Pretty much."

I glanced back to the wall, as proud of her as I ever had been. Then, tucked in the corner of the mirror was a newspaper clipping highlighting the championship we'd won the night Travis and I had her in Coach's office. Travis was beside me, smiling right along with the rest of the team as we celebrated our win.

"I'll never forget that night," she said quietly.

I turned and went to her, no longer willing to keep any distance between us. I wrapped my arms around her waist and pinned her against me.

She gazed up at me, her cool blue eyes ravaging my heart. "I had dreamed of you so many nights. Right here. And then, like a dream, you came true."

I wove my fingers through her hair, in awe of everything about her right now. "And I failed you."

She shook her head. "You were everything I dreamed, and so much more."

"You gave me everything," I whispered.

She nodded.

"Do you regret it?"

I waited not so patiently for her answer. God, if she regretted what I put us through it would gut me beyond repair.

"I don't regret a minute of it. But things have to change, Eric. This has been an intense year. Being with you...it's all-consuming. I've loved you longer than you've even known my name. And because I have, I gave you all my trust from day one."

"Tell me how I can earn it back. I'll give you anything. Anything, Clare..."

"If there's only room for two of us in this relationship, we have to leave jealousy and lies at the door. You have to promise me that."

"I promise," I murmured. "I fucked up. I couldn't stomach the thought of you being with that guy."

"I wasn't with him."

I frowned and then released the tension as the truth hit me. All the sordid imaginings of him fucking her had become nightmares for me. Now they disappeared knowing that she hadn't spent the weekend in his bed.

"You didn't see him?"

"I did, but we decided that we were better off as friends. I talked to Paul too. He knows friendship has to be enough, otherwise we can't have anything."

I exhaled heavily. "So it's just us."

She didn't answer. She only lifted against me and pressed her mouth to mine. The smallest gesture released the animal in me that had craved her body for days. I kissed her deeply and possessively as I pushed her down to the bed.

I stripped her down quickly. I spread her legs and stared at the beautiful wet petals of her pussy.

"Goddamn, you're so beautiful."

My mouth watered at the prospect of tasting her arousal, but my cock was ready to burst if I didn't get inside her. She bit her lip and bowed off the bed slightly. I growled and took the space between her thighs, not wasting another precious second getting inside her.

She gasped when our bodies joined with a hard jolt. I froze there, deeply embedded in her. Suddenly I was breathless with the singular pleasure of being nestled inside her perfect pussy.

"Clare...look at me."

She opened her eyes to half-mast.

"Every time I'm here..." I thrust gently. "I remember how you felt the first time. So perfect. So welcoming of everything I wanted to give you."

I began slow and steady drives that brought us together.

"And I knew from that moment no one would ever make me feel that way. I knew you were special. That together, *we* were special."

Her lip trembled when she said my name. I drove harder, intent on banishing her tears. Her tight pussy added the perfect friction over my cock. I wanted to fuck her hard and come harder, but I was too enraptured with the gift of having her in my arms again. I held her stare, desperate to witness her pleasure, needing her to recognize how much I loved her in this moment.

However long we made love wasn't long enough. I could have existed on the brink of ecstasy with her forever, but as her climax overtook her, my control slipped. I swallowed her cries, moaning against her sweet mouth through my own release. My lips never left hers in a kiss that simultaneously soothed us through the aftershocks and sparked a new wave of desire.

Then I was hard again, fucking her, loving her...staking claim to the body I'd grown to worship, losing myself inside the only girl I'd ever loved.

EPILOGUE

CLARE

I had lost all control. I knew it.

But sometimes old habits were just too hard to break, some desires too overwhelming to deny. After all, it was Eric's fault for turning me into this person, for giving me a taste of my deepest fantasies. I'd thought I had tamed them when we became exclusive, but I'd been very wrong.

Ridgeville's new head football coach drove me insane with desire. From the time I woke up, until the time I went to bed, he consumed my every thought. My body craved him in a way I couldn't explain.

Tonight, I was treading on dangerous territory, risking so much. But no matter how much was at stake, I wasn't backing out.

As I rounded the corner, I set my eyes on my prize and adjusted my scandalously short skirt until it was barely covering my ass. Taking a deep breath, I stepped inside the open threshold and knocked on the doorframe. As reality set in, a wave of panic surged through me. Even if I wanted to, it was too late to back out now.

"Excuse me, Coach? I was wondering if you had a minute."

The handsome new coach sitting at his desk let out an audible gasp. His eyes instantly darkened with desire as he scanned every inch of my body. I trembled when his gaze locked again with mine. The intensity in his stare was beyond exhilarating.

Goddamn, this man was fierce.

Slowly, the corners of his perfect mouth lifted, rewarding me with a heart-stopping grin. "Of course, Clare. Come on in."

I stepped in and shut the door behind me. Making my way across the room, I twisted my hips provocatively with every step toward him. Once I reached the edge of the desk, I stuck my hand out, purposefully knocking his playbook off onto the floor.

"Oh, I'm so sorry." I blinked my eyes at him. "Here, let me get that for you." I took my time, slowly bending over to give him a good view of my bare ass.

"Goddamn." He shifted in his chair.

I placed the book back on his desk with a smirk before dropping to my knees in front of him. I ran my hands up his legs until I felt his erection beneath my fingertips.

Staring up into his soft brown eyes, my breath caught.

God, my husband was a gorgeous man.

Since the day he and I had made our relationship exclusive four years ago, we hadn't been able to keep our hands off each other. Even though our sex life was beyond incredible, we still liked to play out our fantasies on each other, from time to time. Just last week, I was a very naughty nurse.

"You look stressed." I pouted my lip out. "Maybe I can help you out with that."

I tugged at his buckle and unfastened his jeans with ease. His beautiful thick cock sprang out, causing my pussy to ache beneath my skirt. Puckering my lips, I released a mouthful of saliva over his length, working the moisture down over his shaft.

"Clare, what are you doing?" He panted through every word.

"What I've been wanting to do for a long time. I'm about to fuck the coach."

Through hooded eyes, I studied his face as I took him into my mouth.

He groaned when I took him deeper, sliding his hands into my hair.

I locked my lips in place, creating a tight vacuum around him. Relaxing the back of my throat, I began moving my head up and down.

"God, yes, baby. Suck me just like that."

Tightening my hold around the base of his cock, I pressed my tongue against the sensitive part of his shaft, watching as his head fell back from the sensation. I loved having this kind of control over my husband. When the salty taste of his pre-come hit my tongue, I released him from my mouth. Keeping my eyes locked to his, I reached for him, jerking his tie as I urged him to stand with me.

"Do you have any idea what will happen if we get caught?"

I bit my lip and nodded slowly. Having his cock inside my body was well worth the risks.

In one swift move of his arm, Eric cleared his desk, sending papers and books flying across the room. Grabbing me by the waist, he hoisted me up onto the desk, pressing his hand against my chest to urge me backward. I was drenched for him, aching for him. I didn't care how he took me.

Eric slid his hands beneath my thighs, teasing the top of his dick at my soaked opening. He looked down at me, pinning me with those dangerous dark eyes.

"Tell me what you want, Clare."

"Fuck me, Coach," I writhed beneath him. "I want you to fuck me until I can't breathe."

In one forceful thrust forward, he plunged his cock inside me, pushing through the tight, wet lips of my cunt, not stopping until his mind-blowing length had hit my cervix. He didn't give my body time to adjust before he pulled out and thrust back into me, this time with even more force than before. I let out a strangled cry as I arched against the desk, welcoming his aggressive pace. The sounds of our loud moans reverberating off the office walls triggered the first powerful orgasm.

"Yes, Eric. Yes!" I shouted, throwing my head back against the desk.

Cursing, he pulled out of me, flipping me over onto my stomach.

Lifting up my skirt, he delivered two hard blows across my backside. "Get on your knees, baby."

I gave him a wicked grin, positioning my body on all fours. Eric let out a growl when I pushed my ass up into the air, taunting him.

Grabbing both my wrists, he plunged into me, tugging my arms with each slide of his cock. "Jesus Christ! That sweet little cunt is tight."

"Give it to me, Coach."

"Fuck, Clare. So. Good." He gritted out through each thrust.

"I'm coming. Oh, God. Yes! Yes!" I shuddered against him, feeling the rush of my orgasm rise and fade.

Eric collapsed against me, his cock still pulsing inside me. Panting, he eased himself out, staggering backward until he fell into the leather chair beside his desk.

"You're going to kill me one day, you know that, right?"

I lowered myself back onto the floor and adjusted my skirt. "At least I'd make it fun for you before you died," I teased, earning a chuckle from him. "Besides, don't you feel better after that?"

"Much better." He motioned for me to come to him. I climbed into his lap, straddling him. Placing his hands on my bottom, he squeezed my ass, spreading apart my cheeks. I caught the fiery look that blazed through his eyes. He moved me against him, causing me to gasp at the feel of his hard cock against my swollen clit. His stamina still amazed me.

"Why can't I ever get enough of you?" He breathed, staring back into my eyes.

I wrapped my hand around his black tie and pulled him toward me, brushing my lips against his as I spoke. "It's the same for me. A lifetime of this would never be enough."

He rotated his hips. "Then we better make every second count."

◆ ◆ ◆ ◆

Eight months later...

The referee blew his whistle, allowing Eric to take his final time-out of the game. It was the fourth quarter. Ten seconds remained on the clock. Fourth down, Ridgeville trailed three points behind Trinity High—a longtime rival—in the regional championship game. Only twenty yards separated us from declaring victory. When it came to football, it simply didn't get any tenser than this.

Rubbing my hand over my massive stomach, I glanced over at my husband, who was huddled around by his team and pointing at the play chart in his hand. I didn't handle pressure well. But Eric? Eric lived for moments like these.

A sharp pain shot across my lower back, stealing my breath. My best friend Megan, who was home to attend my baby shower, placed her hand on my arm.

"Are you okay?"

I nodded, wincing as the front part of my swollen belly tightened. "Yeah, I think it's just from sitting on these bleachers. I haven't been able to get comfortable in months."

I was only three days away from my due date. However, according to my doctor's visit earlier that day, I still had not shown any signs of progression, which was fine with me since I still had a ton of things to do before the baby arrived.

From out of nowhere, another pain hit, this time stronger. I grabbed Megan's hand, squeezing as I breathed through the contraction. When it had passed, my best friend eyed me with concern.

"Maybe I should get Eric."

"No, I'm fine. He needs to focus on the game. Besides, I've had Braxton Hicks on and off for a week now. They'll pass." I shifted my weight, trying to ease the uncomfortable feeling in my side.

The whistle blew, indicating the game was resuming. The players took their stance, and everyone in the stadium began stomping their feet. The ball was snapped and both teams sprang to action, running, shoving, colliding. The senior quarterback reached back, looking downfield at the wide receiver, and let it rip. I held my breath as the leather ball sailed through the air.

"Touchdown! Ridgeville!" The commentator's voice boomed across the stadium, just as the buzzer announced the end of the game.

Overwhelmed with excitement, I jumped to my feet. As the crowd rushed the field to celebrate the win, there was a sudden gush of warm liquid falling at my feet, followed by a powerful pain in my side. I fell forward, grabbing the rail in front of me.

"Whoa, I got you," Megan said, wrapping her hand around my shoulders. Just as my head lifted, Eric's eyes locked to mine, his elated expression dropping once he saw me bent over in pain. He pushed his way through the sea of people, leaping over the stairwell to rush to me.

"Clare? Are you okay?"

The returning pain was so intense that my answer came out in a scream.

"We need the paramedics over here now!" He shouted over his shoulder, easing me back down onto the bleachers. Eric's parents, who were sitting on the other side of the stadium with friends, hurriedly made their way over to us.

Eric knelt down in front of me, draping my arms over his shoulders, while his mom began rubbing my lower back.

"Breathe, baby. I'm right here."

A few minutes later, the paramedics had surrounded us, helping me down the flight of stairs. Once I had reached the ground level, I was loaded into the back of an ambulance. Eric climbed in right beside me.

I gazed at him apologetically. "I'm sorry to ruin your night."

He leaned into me, pressing his head against mine. "Are you kidding me? It doesn't get any better than this."

Dr. Leslie Marx, who had become a good friend, was on call at the hospital when we arrived. She met us at the emergency room door with a bright expression.

"This baby sure knows how to make an entrance, I'll say that," she teased, putting on her examination gloves to check me. I winced as she measured the opening of my cervix with her fingers. When I glanced back at her, she was grinning.

"You ready to push this kid out?"

"What?" I gasped. "But what about my epidural?"

"You're already fully dilated. I'm afraid there's not going to be enough time for that."

A tall nurse approached her, holding out a blue surgical gown. Leslie reached her arms through the front and situated herself on a stool in between my legs. I couldn't understand why everything was happening so fast. Wasn't labor supposed to last longer than this?

"Okay, Clare. On your next contraction, I want you to bear down in your bottom and push as hard as you can, all right?"

She barely had gotten the words out when I felt another contraction hit. I tightened my hold on Eric's hand.

"Oh, God!" I screamed as the intense pain ripped through me.

"Here we go. Take a deep breath, and push!"

Tucking my chin to my chest, I pushed against the pressure in my bottom until I was completely out of air. I dropped my head back against the pillow, struggling to refill my lungs. Eric wiped my sweaty locks away from my face, kissing me on the forehead. "You're doing great, baby."

Another pain.

"Push, push, push," Leslie coached from in front of me.

There was an agonizing shift in my pelvis.

"Oh, my God. I can see him, Clare! He's got a head full of dark hair!" Eric exclaimed.

"You've got this, girl. Just keep your breathing steady. One more good push, and we'll have a baby." Leslie smiled up at me.

The returning pressure was so intense that I thought I was going to rip apart. I was so desperate for relief. Bearing down hard, I let out a bloodcurdling scream, feeling the baby's shoulders pass through. Then, instant euphoria overtook me as I heard my son's beautiful cry fill the room.

Eric was beaming as he cut the umbilical cord, captivated by every sound and move our son made. Leslie finished up on me while they checked the baby's vitals, which, judging by how well his lungs worked, were healthy. When Eric finally placed him in my arms, I couldn't stop the tears from falling. I feathered kisses across his perfect chubby face, mesmerized by every beautiful feature. His nose, his chin, his mouth, everything was a carbon copy of his father.

"He's so perfect," I breathed, looking back up at Eric, who was staring at me with so much love in his eyes.

"Yes, he is... Just like his mother."

MORE MISADVENTURES

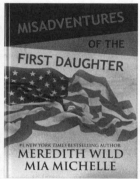

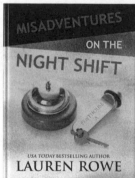

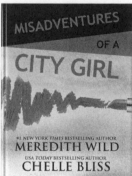

MORE MISADVENTURES

VISIT MISADVENTURES.COM
FOR MORE INFORMATION!

ABOUT M.F. WILD

M.F. Wild is the inappropriate, uninhibited, and slightly embarrassing alter-ego of #1 *New York Times* bestselling author Meredith Wild. When she gets bored of writing emotionally charged love stories, she teams up with her favorite partners in crime to pen the steamiest tales their twisted imaginations can come up with. She enjoys short walks on the beach (because Florida is hot), margaritas, and her husband.

VISIT HER AT MEREDITHWILD.COM!

ABOUT MIA MICHELLE

Mia fell in love with the literary world at a very young age and began putting her active imagination to pen and paper by the age of six. Over the years, she has filled up numerous shelves with her notebooks and journals of her favorite stories. Twelve years ago, Mia began drafting The Thorne Series and through encouragement of a close friend, decided to finally take the leap of faith to bring her dream to life. She openly admits to having a hopeless infatuation with her Kindle and suffers from the one-click book addiction (No intervention required).

Mia Michelle resides in Tennessee with her soul mate and husband of 18 years and their 2 beautiful young children.

VISIT HER AT MIAMICHELLEAUTHOR.COM!